TARGET EARTH

THE EMILY SMITH TRILOGY, BOOK 3

TOM YOUNG

Target Earth
The Emily Smith Trilogy Book 3
All Rights Reserved.
Copyright © 2021 Tom Young
v1.0 r1.2

This is a work of fiction. Names, characters, businesses, places, events, locales, and incidents are either the products of the author's imagination or used in a fictitious manner. Any resemblance to actual persons, living or dead, or actual events is purely coincidental.

The opinions expressed in this manuscript are solely the opinions of the author and do not represent the opinions or thoughts of the publisher. The author has represented and warranted full ownership and/or legal right to publish all the materials in this book.

This book may not be reproduced, transmitted, or stored in whole or in part by any means, including graphic, electronic, or mechanical without the express written consent of the publisher except in the case of brief quotations embodied in critical articles and reviews.

Outskirts Press, Inc.
http://www.outskirtspress.com

ISBN: 978-1-9772-3536-7

Cover Photo © 2021 www.gettyimages.com. All rights reserved - used with permission.

Outskirts Press and the "OP" logo are trademarks belonging to Outskirts Press, Inc.

PRINTED IN THE UNITED STATES OF AMERICA

Contents

1. UGLY SURPISE 1
2. INCURSION 5
3. LATE SECURITY WARNING 7
4. ON STATION 11
5. HANLEE'S DARING ADVENTURE
   TWENTY-FIVE DAYS BEFORE INVASION 14
6. FATHER AND DAUGHTER CAMPING 20
7. WHERE IS HANLEE 24
8. HANLEE'S REVELATION 27
9. INTELLIGENCE INSERTION 33
10. ENGAGEMENT ASSESSMENT 36
11. EMILIES PORCH
    (TWENTY DAYS BEFORE INVASION) 40
12. BECKY'S FEAR
    (FIFTEEN DAYS BEFORE INVASION) 43
13. WARREN JR.'S HEART 47
14. TRANSCENDENCE 52
15. A SHARED HEART 54
16. A GRAND MOTHER'S SOLEMN JOY 60
17. SECOND CHANCE 64
18. THANK YOU FOR LOVING ME 68
19. CREATION'S MISTY REALM 73
20. MESSAGE FROM AFAR 80
21. FIRST TEARS OF DEPARTURE
    (TEN DAYS BEFORE INVASION) 86

22.	WARREN JUNIOR'S CHALLENGE	93
23.	EXCITING EXCUSION	98
24.	HIGH SCHOOL OUTING DELIGHT SEVEN DAYS BEFORE INVASION	106
25.	ENLIGHTEN THE LEADERSHIP	110
26.	STRANGE VISITORS	113
27.	MUTUAL FRIENDS	116
28.	MEETING OF ANGELS	123
29.	A TIME TO WEEP, A TIME TO MOURN	129
30.	MESSAGES RECEIVED	133
31.	PREPARING DEFENSE	139
32.	FLATA'S FEAR	146
33.	TWO DAYS BEFORE INVASION COMING TO AGREEMENT	151
34.	DESPERATE MEASURES	159
35.	UNPLANNED BAPTISM OF FIRE (INVASION DAY)	165
36.	PRAYERS UNCEASING	176
37.	COUNTER ATTACK IN THE VOID OF SPACE	182
38.	IMMENENT ENEMY ARRIVAL	189
39.	CHANGE OF FATE	198
40.	NIGHT TERROR	202
41.	WAITING NO LONGER	208
42.	FIRST ENGAGEMENT	216
43.	LAST CLASS	223
44.	PAIN OF LOSS	229
45.	PRELUDE TO FINAL ENGAGEMENT	233
46.	A TIME TO WEEP, A TIME TO MOURN	237
47.	MIRACULOUS APPEARANCE	242
48.	HANLEE'S MISSION	248

49. EVACUATION	252
50. A PRIVILEGE TO SERVE	259
51. WITNESS	262
52. NEW DAWN, DAY ONE	266
53. THE LAST SUNRISE	269

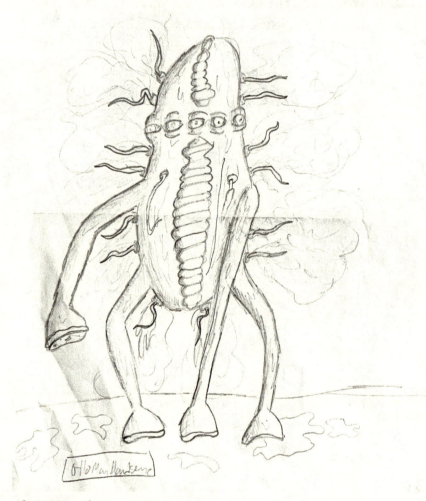

Alien Drawn by Forrest Young

CHAPTER 1
UGLY SURPISE

Kyla sat on her lounge chair on the beach looking out over the white sand that slipped gently beneath the waves as they frothily slathered up onto the shore. The water a short distance from the shore was an absolute calm. She was thinking how odd it was that she had not seen Emily Smith for at least ten years, yet she had seen Sara at least four times a year. Some of the time she was with Jawane, a real odd duck, but mostly she was alone. She seemed to have hardened in ways she could not understand.

Sara had always told me to "be prepared to leave on a moment's notice." Leave where? And, why leave at all? Their contracting business with the military had made all of them rich beyond their wildest dreams.

"Ha, not that they had time to enjoy the largess", mused Kyla.

Kyla adjusted her large bonnet and shielded her eyes as she focused on some kind of disturbance about fifty yards from the shore. She was fairly certain that it was not a large fish because the area of disturbance was just too large and wide.

Looking toward her ten-year-old twins playing near the water's edge Kyla called out to them, "Haley! Paul! Come here to me please! It is important!"

Both children obeyed their Mother and ran up to her.

"What do you want Mom? We do not have to go yet, do we?", intoned Paul.

Kyla looked again at the disturbed water which was now only about twenty-five yards away from the beach.

Kyla stood up and called out to the other young children playing in and near the water's edge; She had an uneasy feeling about the disturbance in the water; it just did not look natural.

"Children! Get out of the water now! Come away now!"

Other parents became aware of Kyla's warning and scrambled to their feet to collect their children.

There was a loud scream as one of the children cried out in pain, then another child, and yet another! The water's edge had become a roiling mass of withering black bodies of the likes of which Kyla had never seen!

A man ran to the water to retrieve his small son playing in the sand and the man appeared to be burned in half by some kind of water jet; his body smoked as it fell down and he screamed, withering in pain thrashing his arms uselessly in the sand. His small son dissolved in a pile smoking flesh as the burning liquid spewed over his body. The bones were still sitting erect as the flesh flowed from his frame.

The black undulating mass became individual creatures with four appendages which extended from the front and the rear and to the sides, a row of eyes encircling around its head. There were large red swollen membranes all over the body from which small snake like appendages sprayed the burning liquid.

Kyla grabbed her children by the arms and began to drag them from the beach. The speed of the undulating mass increased exponentially and seemed to be just yards away. One of the creatures stood on the bottom two appendages and appeared to be preparing to spray her and the children.

Kyla was terrified, and she knew that if she was so much as touched by the liquid, she would not be able to get away. Also, in that moment an impossible thought flashed thru her mind as she remembered Sara continuously admonishing her to always be prepared to leave on a moment's notice. Sara must have been aware of these creatures! That was what all the military contracts were about!

As Kyla stumbled backward the ugly creature shot a thick, steaming, gelatinous stream toward her and just as quickly someone or something dove in front of her and was firing a laser rifle at the ugly disgusting blob. The liquid hit the individual in the chest area and Kyla heard a loud singeing.

Just as fast as the individual dove in front of Kyla, five commandoes reached the individuals side, scooped up the individual and began backing away all the while firing their lasers into the undulating blobs!

Kyla felt her arms being jerked up and then observed she was airborne and landing in a net device about thirty yards from her previous position. Haley and Paul quickly followed behind landing squarely within the net which became a cocoon. It was then she observed numerous saucers and helicopter type craft, and individual self-propelled soldiers dancing in the air firing not only lasers, but some kind of gel gun that caused the ugly beings to become immobile.

Kyla thought, "Flying saucers! Really! Well why not, there are these ugly creatures dissolving people with some kind of liquid acid!"

Kyla and the children were released from the net and ushered to the side the saucer going down the twenty-foot wide ramp, by a military member dressed in a type of uniform of which she was not familiar.

Kyla then saw a gravity assist medical transport device being loaded on the same saucer as she and her twins were standing next to. She had never seen one of those either. The device contained the body of a woman who was writhing in pain. Medical attendants were filling the device with some kind of white cloud substance that hardened quickly. It was then, to her astonishment, she saw Sara staring up at her with a grimaced smile on her face as she disappeared within the cloud.

CHAPTER 2
INCURSION

Muskula was sitting at her console in the underwater marine station that ran surveillance on the lake area. The Andrians had developed a sophisticated sonar system that allowed the sentries on duty to observe visually to an underwater distance of ten miles. The listening devices also amplified the already acute hearing of the aquatic species. They could identify sounds up to twenty miles away without hearing devices.

Muskula froze in her chair as she heard an all too familiar sound of water being displace creating thousands of air bubbles. Then the familiar static sound that the enemy blobs made communicating with one another. She knew the rising decibel and intensity of the static indicated the arrival of an ever-increasing number of the enemy.

Muskula was astounded. The sounds indicated that the number was innumerable.

"How was that possible? How did they get here without being detected?"

Muskula pushed the alarm button that notified Space Intelligence that an attack was underway. At the same time, she alerted all the patrols and sentries that were scattered thru out the great lake and beach head, the location and distance of the incursion.

Muskula and her mate grabbed their new and

improved lightening weapons and dove into the water. They boarded a carrier with several other members of their group and the carrier, along with many others, sped toward the beach under water.

Muskula was the first out and immediately started firing at the alien incursion that they all knew was going to happened but hoped in their heart of hearts that it could be prevented. Muskula did not have time to wonder what happened to Emily and her friends as she put all her energy and concentration into destroying as many of the enemy aliens as possible.

Being underwater was their element and they could easily out maneuver the enemy aliens and with their new weapons they killed untold thousands; and to their relief it seemed like the endless spigot of alien flow was cut off and they only had to contend with those toward the beach.

It was this under water battle that had caused the surface disturbance that Kyla had seen. The battle was fierce and over two hundred feet deep. The engagement had delayed the alien's approach to the beach long enough to allow a response from the space intelligence commandoes to reach the beach and be effective, but not for all. There were over one thousand people on the beach at the time of the attack. The casualties of civilians were at least half; however, by military standards, one was too many. How did the enemy slip past the space intelligence's vigilant surveillance net?

CHAPTER 3
LATE SECURITY WARNING

Sara put her coffee cup down and picked up the intelligence briefing that was marked "URGENT". It had come in within the last two minutes. The sentries at Lagrange Point Station Two had noted a disturbance in the star field that lasted for about three minutes. They had not seen any craft or undue light that seemed to be alarming. In fact, the report noted that should it had only lasted for a few seconds the initial sentry that saw it would think nothing of it at all and in all probability, would not have reported it to Space Intelligence believing it was just his imagination.

Since Ensign Robert Aaron had been abducted from the space station, the living quarters had been enlarged fourfold and now was manned by a crew of four. Thus, all four members had observed the star field anomaly and collectively believed it was possibly an incursion into Human space by the alien enemy, thus they sent out the alert and also prepared to abandon the station in the escape saucers provided for just such on occasion.

Minutes after receiving the security threat notice from Lagrange Point Station Two, Muskula sounded the alarm from the deep-sea ocean watch station that confirmed that an attack was in progress and provided the coordinates for the incursion.

Sara sounded the alarm in the command center and ran to her saucer already dressed in combat gear which included the new acid resistant coveralls, laser pistol, and a small automatic shoulder laser which fired where one was looking. The tight metallic cap on her head picked up the electrical impulses from her optic nerves, and automatically operated the weapons.

Once seated in the control seat of the bio mechanical Entity, Sara's mind was infused and coalesced with the Entity. The Entity advised the exact same location of the incursion and also informed her of her friend Kyla's location. They were one and the same.

Sara, being in command of the unit advised, "Land as soon as possible and open fire. Do not worry about being observed by the populace. We need to save as many of them as possible."

The saucer landed and Sara hit the sand running. Her personal locator showed Kyla's position and she ran in the direction indicated, all the while firing her laser at the alien enemy that was attacking on the beach.

Sara saw Kyla dragging her two children away from the beach being followed by one of the alien beings which was standing up preparing to spew its acid on them. Sara raced with all her might and just managed to dive in front of Kyla as the alien being spewed its deadly acid. The acid hit Sara squarely in the chest burning the acid resistant suit almost thru. Some of the acid did penetrate the suit and even the few drops that

TARGET EARTH

did caused severe pain and burning. The burning of the caustic acid took her breath away as Sara fired her weapon cutting the alien in half. Sara hit the sand and immediately she was picked up by four members of her commando team who rushed her to a field medical isolator which filled with jell to hold her in place and infuse her with healing nutrients and morphine-based medication to stabilize her until she could be transported to the hospital.

Sara looked up with pain filled eyes as the white cloud began filling the medical isolator with the white gas that turned to jell. She saw Kyla looking down at her with her mouth open and her eyes big. Sara gave a grimaced laced smile as the gas covered her face and she mercifully went to sleep.

At the same time that Lagrange Point Station 2 notified Space Intelligence on the ground, the alert was sent to the five intergalactic carriers that was assigned to guarding the earth for just such an occasion.

The carriers pinpointed the location of the star field disturbance and all five fired simultaneously their most powerful weapons creating an enormous black hole that swallowed up huge sections of space.

Their sensors could see that an innumerable number of the enemy ships were vaporized as they were crushed down to the smallest atoms. The fleet searched for any other enemy but was unable to locate any more of their ships.

The disturbance in the heavens was easily seen from the surface of the earth. There was first a large blast of light brighter than the sun and then it quickly disappeared into a black hole that seem to diminish in size as it raced away from the vicinity of earths space.

CHAPTER 4
ON STATION

Emily, Blain and Sasha stood in the command center after arriving at the coordinates provided by the captain of the Intergalactic Carrier that had been battling the alien fleet for the past several months. Nothing they did seem to deter them from their predetermined course, Earth.

The Captain had sent communications advising that they had finally been able to learn the communication channels of the chain of command and were in the process of working to destroy their capabilities.

Emily observed the 3D holovision of the Captain who was cocooned within a command unit.

"We have been changing our coordinates every few minutes when we engage them. We have learned to scan the cosmos for disturbances within the star field which is an indicator that they are jumping to our location. We move quickly and have observed vast numbers of their species dump into outer space from the time warp. They do not live long and some even burst into flames."

"I do not even have a guess of how many of their ships we have sent into black holes and have observed them explode outward first then implode with the gravitational field crushing them into fine dust. I just do not know where they all come from."

Emily looked at the captain and could see the weary and worn out look of someone who is battle fatigued. There was no safety here. She heard an alarm sound in the background and the Captain said, "Gotta run, we will make contact later". Then the holovid went dead.

Emily contacted the ten Neanderthal crew mates that had the gift of remote viewing and advised them meet in the special viewing room that had a ceramic glass wall. This area had been redesigned to enable those involved in remote viewing to be connected to the bio-mechanical Entity living within the Intergalactic Carrier. Using her internal communicator Emily contacted the Captain of the Bridge;

"Captain, watch for star field disturbances on a three-hundred-and-sixty-degree spherical arc. If nothing is noted, move the Carrier to new jump coordinates every fifteen minutes varying the jump time plus or minus five minutes. And if star field indicators show signs of displacement and incoming aliens are imminent, move immediately, then begin random jumping every three minutes."

"Yes Commander", replied the Captain of the Bridge.

Blain advised, "We have lost one Intergalactic Carrier with all five thousand crewmen. Somehow the aliens have mastered the science of interspatial translation."

Sasha responded, "It appears they work as a cohesive whole building upon each other's thoughts and insights. And, being connected physically allows them instantaneous transfer of knowledge within their ships, then the collective knowledge is transmitted thru out the fleet with the electrical discharges. The communication works both ways. Somehow, we need to ground the static charges to prevent intra ship communications, maybe that will slow them down, or maybe better yet, we could lead them into a black void!"

CHAPTER 5
HANLEE'S DARING ADVENTURE TWENTY-FIVE DAYS BEFORE INVASION

Hanlee's Friday morning class was one of her favorites. All the students were engaged in math, science, and chemistry. She was looking forward to her weekend as she was going to go camping.

She wasn't really one-hundred percent focused on her lecture as part of her mind was preoccupied about her upcoming weekend. And as she was lecturing Hanlee stated, "...the Humans have occupied the space station around Saturn's largest moon, Titan, now for at least eight years...". Before she continued on, one of the students raised his hand and said, "Excuse me, but you said, "The Humans" occupied the space station around Saturn's moon Titan. I mean, who else could possibly occupy any space station in our solar system?"

Hanlee looked like a dear caught in the head lights and was startled with the question. She actually said Humans occupied the Space Station.

Hanlee thought quickly and said, "That was a good

catch! I want you to look at it as if per chance you are an alien race coming into the solar system and you found Humans on the space station. Exactly how do you think the Humans would react?"

No one said anything because it was such an odd turn of events for their science class.

"Well a dear friend of mine told me that the way Humans should react toward aliens is by....Pointing one finger up on each side of your head like "this," demonstrating how to do so, then she danced in a circle singing, "We are Humans from Earth! Take us to your leader!"

As she said that she continued dancing in a circle singing the same song that Emily had taught her when she was a child. Hanlee laughed and ran in the circle three times singing the song circling the entirety of the large theater stage.

All the students sat startled by Hanlee's antics because up to this very moment she had been very shy, demure, and rarely smiled. Soon one student then another got up and ran forward and joined Hanlee in the circle dance singing the same song. It only took seconds before the whole class left their seats and joined in the light-hearted frolic of their professor. They all laughed in the spontaneous comradery of a previously serious class. Everyone left the class room laughing and talking as Hanlee thoughtfully watched them go.

"They were such good young people. They had no animosity in their hearts and they loved learning and loved life. They deserved to live," Thought Hanlee. Hanlee closed her brief case and slowly walked from the building.

Hanlee dressed slowly after a leisure shower. Since being on the Earth for almost 10 years she never took any other kind. She knew in her heart that if there were not any changes on the Intergalactic Carriers there was no way she would willingly go back to living on one. Of course, the caveat is "willingly".

Thinking about Emily she became somewhat despondent. They all have become worried about not hearing anything from Emily since she, Blain, and Sasha, left on an Intergalactic Carrier to do battle with the Eighth Dimension entity that was destroying all carbon base life forms in the known universe.

They had been gone for almost ten years and no one had heard a word. The Andrian fleet had sent messages from time to time stating that they have done battle with small pockets of the invaders but they had no knowledge of where the nucleus of the invaders innumerable host has disappeared too.

Hanlee knew all too well that with the Intelligent Entities within the Saucers and Carriers, and the Intergalactic Carriers ability to travel thru different dimensions and space time itself, that it was possible they would never see Emily and the others ever again. That thought brought pain to her soul and tears to her eyes. Surely, they must be in constant battle with the enemy. They were reportedly as numerous as the sands of the sea.

Hanlee put the heavy thoughts aside and walked out the door of her bungalow. She was now a professor of mathematics at a small rural college about seventy-five miles South of their home base. Hanlee chose this particular school because she believed there was a small pocket of Humans that exhibited a higher degree of intelligence and were very aggressive in their search for knowledge. Her brother Jawane and she had taught mathematics nightly on a VO VID station set up by Space Intelligence to help locate gifted students. For some unexplained reason, many of the listening population was from this area and were enrolled in this small college.

Hanlee had obtained a teaching position at the college and searched diligently for any student that offered promise of higher analytical math and science skills. The ones she found were added to the list of possible transferees to an Intergalactic Carrier that was designated as an ark. There were ten Arks or carriers around the moon in the event it was necessary to evacuate quickly should the enemy reach the earth. The enemy could be destroyed but there was not enough "bullets" to destroy the never-ending stream of invaders.

Being exhausted from a week of twelve-hour days and a long semester, Hanlee had decided to do something entirely different and completely out of the box for her, she was going camping. She had a small tent, a compass, military food rations, several jugs of water, a small knife, and of course, a small Andrian laser blaster that would fit in the palm of her hand. After notifying Sara of her intentions and giving her destination coordinates, Hanlee got into her small vehicle and hit the road eagerly looking forward to her first ever visit to the Adirondack State Park.

Hanlee set up camp by a pristine stream which had a twenty-foot bank and the water rushed into Lake Ontario, although due to its depth, it seemed to be at a leisurely pace. She was the only one around. Exhausted, Hanlee sat her folding lounge chair beneath the tree next to the tent, and quickly went to sleep. This particular schedule was followed for the next three days and was a prelude to night viewing of the clear sky with her small star scope.

On the fourth day Hanlee was alerted to someone's presence by her personal security monitors which she had placed around her camp site.

Four men emerged thru the foliage. They were heavily armed, bearded and dressed in military cameo uniforms. They were not her security team nor were they wearing known military insignias.

Hanlee's heart gave an alarming uptick as she assessed her ability to defeat the four men without killing them out right with her laser pistol. Reading their minds, all of them had distressingly evil thoughts against her. She did not possess the martial arts skills exhibited by Emily and Sara. She never believed that she would place herself in such a position where they were needed. And, she usually had a military guard around her. She chose to dispense with one for the weekend outing. It was evident to her now that that was a lack of good judgement.

Using her mind Hanlee said, "I am of no interest to you, go away."

One of the four men turned around and started walking away. One stood still looking confused. The other two showed no indication that they heard her command.

Before she could move the man closest to her hit her squarely in the face breaking her nose. Hanlee was stunned. She stumbled backward trying to keep her balance as she landed upright against a large tree.

The man was upon her in an instant clawing at her blouse and kissing her hard. She had never known a man and she was terrified. Struggling, she managed to knee him hard in the groin stopping the attack momentarily. Turning, Hanlee stumbled thru the brush to the possible safety of the stream. She was almost to the streams bank when she felt or rather heard a loud whack. Hanlee was knocked unconscious by the man wielding a small, stout, tree limb.

Hanlee fell head first over the embankment to the rushing stream twenty feet below. She hit the water unconscious and was swept away by the swift current. The two men above on the embankment looked in dismay as their would-be midnight entertainment floated out of sight around a small bend.

CHAPTER 6
FATHER AND DAUGHTER CAMPING

Ricky and his daughter Tiffany were enjoying a Father-Daughter outing of camping and fishing. They had been there two days and were ready to return home. Tiffany looked out over the water and saw what she believed at first to be a small log but to her dismay was really a body.

"Dad! Dad!, there is a body floating over there." Ricky looked up in time to see the body float about twenty more feet as it moved swiftly down-stream.

Running into the rapid moving water Ricky grabbed the arm of a young woman and dragged her to the shore before picking her up and laying her down in the grass. She was unconscious and was not breathing. Ricky quickly began giving her mouth to mouth resuscitation and chest compressions. He observed that her blouse had already been torn off with the buttons still attached. Then he noticed the bleeding from the back of her head.

Ricky shouted to his daughter, "Get the gun, stand guard, she has been attacked!"

Tiffany, not needing to be told twice ran to the tent and retrieved a handgun with which she was very proficient. She took up a stance about twenty feet away and faced the bank foliage.

"Is she going to be alright Dad?"

Ricky continued to administer CPR and after several more breaths, the young woman rolled over to her side and threw up copious amounts of water. Falling on her back again, Hanlee looked up into the concerned brown eyes of a young man about her age. He was really cute.

Saying out loud, "Wow, I must have been hit harder than I thought."

The back of her head felt like it was splitting in two. She rubbed her head and brought her hand away covered in blood. Hanlee then remembered the two of the four men that attacked her. What happened to them?

Noticing then that her blouse was not only opened exposing her breast but there was a warm hand print of the man who had saved her, imprinted on her chill bumped breast. Hanlee hurriedly covered herself and her face flushed deep red. Thinking to herself, she intoned, again out loud, "I guess I am more assimilated than I thought".

Ricky had no idea what she was talking about and assumed it was the bump on the head that made her speak strange things. He did observe that she was nicely built and very attractive even though she behaved in some strange demure way.

"Is she alright Dad? Is she going to be okay?" Tiffany walked closer to them so she could look at the woman but she did not let her guard down as she continually scanned the foliage for possible attackers.

Hanlee observed that the young woman with the hand gun was really a girl about thirteen years of age.

She was wearing cutoff blue jeans and a sleeveless tank top with some band's name on it. She had short blonde hair the same color as her Dads.

Hanlee thought a minute then she said, "What was I talking about when I said I must be really assimilated? Where am I and what am I doing here?"

Ricky saw the confusion register on the woman's face and he said, "Tiffany saw you floating by in the water and called out to me in time to rescue you before you passed out of reach. Do you know who attacked you? How many were there? Oh, by the way, my name is Ricky. This is my daughter Tiffany", indicating to the young girl that was holding the gun watching their surroundings.

Hanlee tried to sit up but fell back with a splitting head ache of the kind which she had never known.

Ricky reached for her and helped ease her back down to the grass. "Take it easy, that is quiet a nasty gash you got on the back of your head. If you tell me your name, we can contact someone that could help you. We will be glad to take you to the hospital. However, it is about a three-hour drive from here."

Hanlee looked up and said, "My name is uh, my name is uh". Hanlee looked terrified.

"I cannot remember my name!", said Hanlee in a small soft voice.

Tiffany said, "Let's take her home with us Dad, then we can find out who she is and contact someone she knows."

Ricky replied and said, "Pack our gear and let us get out of here before whoever tried to kill her come back around and find us. I have no doubt they would kill us too."

After quickly packing their gear into their pickup truck, they helped Hanlee to the truck and made her as comfortable as possible. Ricky stayed on the main road using the premise that Hanlee's attackers would not want to be found and thus they would use the back roads. They did not run into the men that attacked Hanlee.

Ricky and Tiffany lived on a small forty-acre piece of land that backed up to the Adirondack State Park, and, like Emily's perfect hideaway, provided the same seclusion. Ricky too had inherited it from his parents.

As they drove into the long drive way they were met by a large German Shepherd which Ricky kept as security for the homestead when they were away and of course being one of the family when they were at home. Once inside, they helped Hanlee to a bed where they cleaned and dressed her wound. Hanlee could not sit up and was exhausted so she was fast asleep. The large Shepherd named Beau, laid down on the bed at her feet and did not leave her side.

Ricky and Tiffany searched the young women's pockets and found nothing except a strange palm sized object with a small hole on one end. They set it on the table. She had nothing but the shirt which was torn and ripped apart by the perpetrator that wished to do her harm and her dungaree jeans. The scratches on her breast were superficial. However, it was apparent that her nose was broken and would need medical attention. It was already too late to drive to town and soon it would be dark and very uncomfortably cold.

CHAPTER 7
WHERE IS HANLEE

Hanlee's security detail began to get nervous when Hanlee had not checked in as planned every six hours. When she missed her call time and they were unable to reach her on her communicator, they notified Space Intelligence. When Sara got the message that the security detail had let Hanlee go off into the woods alone, she was beside herself with anger. Normally she could handle her anger but this is the first time someone had failed to do their duty resulting in the possible danger to her family member.

Summoning a twelve-man reconnaissance squad Sara left the base in a small saucer and quickly landed near Hanlee's last know position. The squad crept thru the foliage to the camp sight and around Hanlee's camp sat four men. They were talking about the young woman they had found and were berating one of the men for beating her and throwing her into the river.

Sara walked into the clearing. There was no telling her "no". The men were surprised to find themselves surrounded by twelve armed men and women with their weapons drawn.

"Sara reached down and grabbed the man by the neck that had beaten and reportedly thrown Hanlee into the river. Lifting him off the ground Sara said, "What happened to the woman you found at this camp sight?"

The man barely being able to speak replied, "She kicked me in the groin and made me mad so I threw her in the river".

Sara could read the man's mind and knew he was lying. She knew he had attacked Hanlee and she fought back kicking him in the groin after he had broken Hanlee's nose. He knocked her up against the tree and ripped her blouse open in an ongoing effort to rape her. When Hanlee tried to flee he hit her in back of the head with a stout branch at which time she fell into the swiftly moving water twenty feet below the bank.

Sara looked at the man for a moment then reaching up with her left hand, she twisted his head around and tore it from his shoulders and pitched it in the middle of the three men still seated frozen in position by the camp fire.

Upon dropping the man, she walked to the other three men who were terrified staring at their friend's head which had rolled in front of them. Reading their minds, she located the second man that was instrumental in attacking Hanlee. She pulled out her laser and without another word she blasted his head to vapor.

The other two men began to stutter and deny having anything to do with the death of the young woman saying they were turning to leave when the other two men proceeded to attack the woman. Sara reading their minds knew they were obeying Hanlee's command to leave.

Turning to an Andrian officer in her detail she said, "Wipe their minds, move them away from here, get them away from me! The rest of us will scour the river bank in an effort to retrieve Hanlee."

Sara's heart ached like it had never ached before and tears of sorrow streamed down her face. She could find no fault with Hanlee's security detail. Hanlee was a grown woman and she could come and go as she pleased. She had been on the earth long enough to take care of herself. And, the instant Hanlee did not call in they notified Space Intelligence.

Sara and her team scrambled down the bank to the water's edge and began searching for any signs of Hanlee. Sara heard a shout as one of the recon team members located what they thought to be evidence of Hanlee's presence. Sara's heart soared when reaching the spot, they found blood on the grass along with several foot prints. It was very possible that Hanlee was alive!

It appeared that someone had found Hanlee in the water and brought her to the bank and performed CPR and first aid to stop the bleeding. There was a full body impression in the grass that was the size of Hanlee. The recon team located tire tracks of a truck and using Andrian technology began following the tracks thru the woods.

CHAPTER 8
HANLEE'S REVELATION

Hanlee was sitting up in bed mumbling something. Ricky and Tiffany went into the bedroom and observed Hanlee sitting cross-legged. She seemed to be in some kind of trance looking straight out in front of her without seeing anything.

Hanlee said," One of the brightest asteroids in the main asteroid belt between mars and Jupiter is the asteroid designated as 2868 Steins, an "E class" asteroid, also known as "a diamond in the sky", because of its unique shape, that being the shape of a diamond. The asteroid was visited by the Earth's Rosetta space craft on September 5, 2008, and has an albedo brightness of .45. However, the Humans later downgraded the asteroid to space debris, once again hiding knowledge from its citizens."

"In effect, it was a large space craft believed to have been a satellite work station that housed thousands of people. It appeared to have been blasted from one side with the skin surface intact on the reflective side. A large circular hole in the top looked to be an access port. It was a remanent of a civilization that once occupied the planet that was blasted to pieces and was now the asteroid belt.

"Uranus's rotational axis is on its side relative to the sun."

"Saturn's moon Hyperion has a small bright green spot in the upper right-hand quadrant of the otherwise dull grey moon as shown in Nasa's photo viewer PIA07740. However, in later pictures the color is extracted and just shows a pinpoint of brightness on the rim of a crater. The green spot is one of our many robotic mining facilities in this solar system."

"Neptune's axis of rotation is twenty-nine degrees relative to the sun and Uranus's moon Miranda, show extensive surface mining furrows. Some furrows exhibit large right angle turns and some are in an oval track setting with various depths. They were present when we first visited this solar system many cycles ago and are of an unknown origin. Nor do we know what minerals they were mining." Then she remained silent.

Tiffany stared at Hanlee with an open mouth. "Dad! Do you know who she is?" Without giving him time to answer Tiffany said, "She is one of the most brilliant teachers of math and science in the whole world! She is on the VU TUBE with her brother. Their faces are always blurred out to preserve their identity. But their math and science skills are phenomenal! I recognize her voice. I would recognize it anywhere!"

"I bet those men who were trying to kill her was doing so to keep her from teaching about the possibility of space travel! Oh Dad! We have to protect her!"

Tiffany ran up to Hanlee and gave her a fierce hug saying, "Oh I love you so much! And you said Earths' Rosetta spacecraft. Whose other space craft are out there. You are not from earth, are you? You are so smart! I just knew you could not be from here, how could you possibly know all those things about the moons and planets if you have not seen them yourself! Will you be my big sister? My very first ever alien friend!"

Both Ricky and Tiffany were startled to suddenly see themselves surrounded by armed men and women with some sort of strange looking rifle... gun, or whatever.

Tiffany turned her back to Hanlee spreading her arms and legs in a protective stance. Beau jumped to all four paws and emanated a low warning growl as he faced the intruders. Ricky stood where he was understanding and knowing all too well there was not anything they could do to protect the young woman he had pulled from the river.

Sara was smiling as she listened to the young girl exclaim her love for Hanlee and proclaiming that she must be an alien and wanting her for a big sister and a friend.

First Sara directed her thoughts to the large German Shepherd and told the dog to be at peace. The Shepherd responded by sitting back down at Hanlee's feet softly whining.

Then addressing the young man and girl, Sara said, "Thank you for saving Hanlee, that is her name. And you are correct. She is the one that teaches on the evening VU programs along with her brother Jawane. And yes, she is from the planet Andria which is two galaxies away from here. However, she herself has grown up on an Intergalactic Carrier and she has not lived on any planet until she came to the planet Earth nearly twenty years ago, right about your age.

Ricky was not so sure that he should be too excited about the information the young woman imparted.

"What are you going to do now, kill us?"

Sara smiled, "I am not sure what to do with you, we certainly are not going to kill you. You helped save someone very precious to me and to us all, indicating the men and women in her unit. I have a wise mentor that said things happen for a reason. You and your daughter happen to be at the precise spot at the precise moment in time to save Hanlee. For whatever reason it appears that you have already been of service to us in a very meaningful way. You exhibited courage when you realized that someone had just tried to kill Hanlee, and yet you did not flee, you administered to her needs. I thank you with all my heart and soul".

Ricky heard the emotion in the woman's voice and saw the glistening of tears in her eyes even though her face for some strange reason seemed hard.

A strange looking woman entered the room and silently examined Hanlee to determine the nature of her injuries. She faced the young woman holding the gun and telepathically told her that Hanlee had a concussion and should be taken to the hospital immediately. Two of the soldiers helped Hanlee up and they walked her outside. Ricky and Tiffany followed behind. They were caught off guard and were aghast to see two flying saucers hovering in their yard. Hanlee was walked up the ramp followed by the strange old lady. The ramp closed and then the saucer shot straight up out of sight.

Sara looked at them and smiled remembering her dad

when he learned about aliens.

"You two seem to be doing well having just learned about aliens. When my dad learned about them, he had to be soothed and put to sleep. But Tiffany, I was a lot like you and at the same age. Life just seemed like a marvelous adventure. And, it has been. I had no idea how marvelous and adventurous it would be. I hope yours will be somewhat less adventuresome, however, I really doubt it."

"The four men that attacked Hanlee have been dealt with. Two are dead and the other two are no longer a threat."

Sara did not expound more on what "no longer a threat", meant. Ricky had observed the blood on Sara's uniform and deemed it would not be wise to inquire.

"Well, if you wish to join us, you are more than welcome. If not, I can have your memories wiped of any knowledge of us. There will be no harm done to you and you may continue to live your idyllic lives here in this currently peaceful valley."

Neither Tiffany nor Ricky liked the dangling inference of "currently peaceful" valley.

"What about Beau? He is part of our family. We could not leave him."

Sara looked at the dog and called it over to her side and ruffled his thick, fury neck. "He can come too. He will fit in nicely. And do not worry about your things. We will pack you up. You can use your home here for a mental health get away, should you ever need one. Perhaps you would not mind if we could all use it from time to time."

Both Ricky and Tiffany `were beside themselves with excitement as they walked up the ramp of the saucer followed by the contingent of soldiers.

CHAPTER 9
INTELLIGENCE INSERTION

Emily, Blain, and Sasha entered the viewing room where everyone was waiting and prepared for the insertion into the alien domain to gather intelligence. No one really knew what to expect. Thy have all experienced remote viewing using the Neanderthal abilities and as amazing and grand as that was it was infinitesimal compared to the combined abilities of the five Entities within the Intergalactic Carriers.

Once seated and cocooned within their respective chambers each closed their eyes and gave in to the Entities sensors inserting themselves into their brains.

And always, as before, Emily could taste and feel the neutrinos and tachyons coursing thru her very spirit, except this time there was a frightening feeling of every particle in her body being aligned in several parallel strings of like molecules. Then she felt Blain, Sasha, Neanderthals, and others in the company arrange themselves in string layers to the side and slightly behind her to create a wedge. The four other ships participants joined together and further increased their numbers changing the wedge into a dense spear of molecules.

Emily directed their flight thru time and space and

soon were in front of the enemy fleet. Emily knew the command ship and they carefully entered thru the hull into the acid laced mist they used for communication in the field. They collectively entered the minds of the command structure and were stunned to find layers and layers of hatred for all carbon life forms imprinted on their essence.

This initial incursion was to find some way to disrupt their communication and redirect their path from the earth and was not intended to be an engagement event. Leaving the command-structure they proceeded farther into the ship where they found millions of their kind lined up in rows with their back packs all pointing in the same direction. The acid mist here was much denser and was dispensed from overhead vents.

Emily then led the arrow to the front of the rows of alien beings as they appeared to be preparing to be launched into some kind of time warp. There was a distinct change of color in the mist and the alien beings appeared to become more agitated and restless as waves of surges and stopes enveloped the whole group.

Emily sensed a wholesale attack was about to be launched toward their fleet and quickly exited the command ship. Emily stretched the arrow across the cosmos in front of the alien fleet and they assumed a glowing likeness of Emily's smiling face laughing haughtily and pointing at the enemy in a dismissive manner.

The ploy seemed to be working as the enemy fleet slowed and bright flashes of effervescent light flashed from the front portals of the enemy ships. Literally millions of alien beings exited the ships landing in the mist of the molecular Emily. Most burst into flames with millions more drifting dead and frozen as the neverending flow of alien bodies dumped into space. The flow continued for an indeterminant time leaving alien body debris floating like an asteroid field or trash upon the sea.

The aliens did not understand what happened to their target but as long as they could see Emily's likeness and she appeared to be present, they were going to do what they could to destroy her. It appeared that once the front fleet a carriers had released and dumped all their soldiers the lead carriers would move out of the way of the next fleet of ships, and then they too would launch their waves of soldiers.

Emily transmitted their coordinates to the five ship captains and commanded them to open fire. Almost immediately there were innumerable flashes of light as large black holes opened in the mist of the enemy fleet.

They too stretched across the cosmos. The fleet of carriers was sucked into the black holes and crushed to extinction as were the bodies of their soldiers as they disappeared into the sucking black holes.

Emily was elated and astonished at their accomplishment when there was no plan in place to engage the enemy. However, looking across the cosmos she could see more of the enemy ships slowly advancing taking the place of the fleets just destroyed. This enemy had one objective and one objective only and that was to destroy all carbon life forms in the human occupied Universe. Emily directed their course to return to their ships.

CHAPTER 10
ENGAGEMENT ASSESSMENT

Upon returning from their excursion, Emily called a conference of all five ships' Captains and crews. Previously the Andrians allowed only the elite "Council of Yield", to join in as a governing body. However, since joining in with Humans they changed their governing model to be more representative of all Andrians with "The Council", being the final arbitrator in decisions relating to the whole fleet. "The Council" now included Humans much to the horror of straggling Andrians resistant to change.

Emily spoke first.

"We have successfully engaged the enemy destroying all that we could. The number of ships and enemy destroyed is innumerable. Should that have been us instead of them we surely would have been annihilated. Obviously, we cannot destroy them all."

"We first encountered them in what we now know as the Eighth Dimension. Prior to that event we were aware of only our dimension. String theory and interdimensional properties were first proposed over a hundred years ago on Earth. However, Andrians have been using the physics before we climbed out of our trees and has allowed them to use string theory and gravity waves to fold time and space for intergalactic travel. Interdimensional travel was not possible until Flata created the machine intelligence within our space craft. Now that intelligence has recreated itself into a super intelligence that surpasses the Andrians. We can only pray that the intelligence within remains benevolent."

"Even though we found the enemy in the Eighth Dimension it is obvious that it did not originate there. Since it is so different from all other known life forms we have encountered and of which we are a part, it must needs be to have come from outside our known universe. If that is the case then it is also true there must also be parallel universes. If the intelligences within our space craft can travel thru time and space then perhaps, they may also travel to a parallel universe. Surely the enemy lifeforms came from one of those parallel universes. Wither they came by accident or by design is of no consequence. Should we not stop them, then all carbon life forms in our known universe will eventually be destroyed."

Blain looked at Emily knowing full well what she was going to do and when she took that course of action, she would be lost to him and their children forever. He did not want to hear her dreaded words that were surely coming. At the same time, he believed it may well be the only way to save their universe, if it could be saved at all.

Emily could read Blains' mind as he could hers. Their pain and grief was shared and Blain took Emily in his arms and placed his forehead against hers. Emily had told Blain about the Hybrid Machine Entity's desire to become one with her. Blain did not know if such a thing was even possible but his experience and observations of Emily and Machine mergence up to this point left him with little doubt that the bio mechanical entity could do whatever it wanted to do. So far the Entity seemed to be controlled by Emily' s strength of will. The question was, would it remain so after they became "one". Emily would no doubt give her life for her loved ones and for all practical purposes, their entire known universe.

"What about the other five entities in the other Intergalactic Carriers? What role will they have in the transition? Will they also be incorporated into One Being or will they remain in their present state?" Blain had so many questions.

"I am beginning to think I am becoming a lot like you in the question arena", Blain said smiling.

"Now I know how you felt when you discovered the access port on Saturn's artifact moon, Hyperion. It was all I could do to keep you from going deeper into artifact to further explore even though I knew it was dangerous to do so."

Emily hugged Blain close and placed her head and cheek up against his chest.

Letting out a long sigh, Emily said, "The only way to find out is to ask the Entity directly. As part of the Entity I can access knowledge about other spheres that may be within the cosmos. I cannot even begin to think about what that will be like or even what I may become."

After the group assessment which did drag on for hours, Emily went to her quarters and fell on her bed and immediately was immersed in a deep sleep. Strange dreams filled her and enveloped her spirit. She dreamed she was a Neutrino travelling through space and she could observe large magnetic waves come and go like swells on a vast ocean. From time to time she could taste different flavors of the swells as the magnetic waves inundated her. Depending on the intensity of the magnetic swells, the flavor of the swells would be that of an electron as it circled thru her being at the speed of light. Sometimes the flavor was of a Muon or a Tau. Each flavor was distinct and moved her into a different sphere of Being. Her speed thru the cosmos would increase or decrease depending upon the flavor of the Atom, Muon, or Tau particle which connected to her Neutrino. From moment to moment, as time had no relevance in this space, she would be attached to a quark and it would be like a burst of blinding energy as she increased her speed through the cosmos.

The Entity then came into her being and said, "That is just a taste of the experiences you will have if you come with me and be "One."

Emily woke with a start. Sweat was streaming down her face and her uniform was soaked with sweat. Up till this moment Emily was not afraid, however now she felt a tinge of fear. She must decide what she was going to do and do it soon.

CHAPTER 11
EMILIES PORCH (TWENTY DAYS BEFORE INVASION)

Hanlee walked out the front door to Emily's porch slamming the screen door behind her. It sounded so good. Emily's home felt like her own home and being there was like a homecoming after so many years away teaching at the college. Her trips back to Emily's have been too few and far between.

Jawane jumped up and rushed to give her a hug.

"Oh Sis, you scared me so much. Surely you know how dangerous it is to go anywhere without your security team!"

And, when he finished the sentence, two men and two women exited the house and took up positions around the perimeter of the porch joining Jawane's security team.

Ricky and Tiffany got up and also greeted Hanlee. However, they were uncomfortable and reticent because they now knew of her celebrity status and they did not know what was or was not acceptable.

Hanlee reading their minds walked over to them and embraced them both in a group hug and tearfully thanked them for saving her life.

"I know that if it was not for your quick action and courage I would not be here today." And Tiffany, "Yes, I would love to be your big sister and your very best "alien", friend ever! In fact, you can be my very best "alien" friend also!"

Everyone laughed at the pun of Tiffany being the alien. Tiffany herself smiled inwardly thinking that was true and she liked the idea of being the alien one.

Jawane spoke up and said, "Tiffany, that means I am your big brother! Although, Ricky, I do not know what that makes us. I guess I could call you Dad!"

Everyone laughed and the comradery was a satisfying stress reliever for both Rickey and Tiffany. It had been a whole week since they had arrived at the compound known as "Emily's House", and they have witnessed many women and men coming and going into the house. Both of them wondered where they went and what they were doing. They had not seen the strange women again, nor had they seen Sara. They had noticed that all the military men and women exhibited extreme deference to her when she was around upon their arrival.

Tiffany was thinking, "Why was that so? Who was she? She seemed so young. I wonder why she does not smile very much?"

Unknown to Tiffany, everyone could read her mind and accept her curious nature. They were all very grateful for their bravery in helping Hanlee.

Hanlee could read their minds also and she colored in her cheeks when Ricky looked at her from across the porch and realized that his look was much more than just a casual glance. He was actually excited by her and vividly recalled placing his hand on her cold, firm breast as he compressed her heart to get it started. He was wondering what it would be like to kiss her full pink lips. It would not have been so distressing if she had not been thinking the exact same thing about him.

One could never accuse the Andrians for being timid. Hanlee walked up to Ricky and ever so slightly kissed his lips, and said, "Thank you for saving my life".

Ricky knew he was hooked and he caught a glimpse of Tiffany beaming a large happy smile in his direction.

They themselves have been staying at a condo about a hundred yards away with a beautiful view of the estuary. Every morning they would get up early and watch the water change colors as the sun came up behind them. Some mornings they would swear they saw large fish fly out of the water in a perfect arc before disappearing beneath the waves. Sometimes the large fish even looked like a person but they both knew that was impossible. It must have been the light.

CHAPTER 12
BECKY'S FEAR (FIFTEEN DAYS BEFORE INVASION)

Becky woke up with a scream on her lips and her heart pounding in her chest. She was covered in sweat. She reached over and found that, as usual, Warren was already off to the forest. She knew his work was important to the environment and it was increasingly apparent that the environment was rapidly changing, and not necessarily for the best. The reports of rising oceans, severe droughts inducing crop failures around the world, torrential rains and other weather phenomena was beginning to make her worried; of course, she knew with Warren and other brilliant scientist working the problem they would soon have the major problems solved.

Still, what was the night terrors about? The thoughts were just beyond her grasp, beneath the surface boiling, surely, they would soon become cognizant thought. Becky pulled her robe about her and checked on Lilly. She was such a delight and smart too, just like her Dad and her brother Warren Junior. Becky tickled Lilly's nose and watched her scratch it not wanting to wake up.

Becky picked Lilly up and walked with her into the

kitchen and set her on a chair. Lilly rubbed her eyes and squinting up at her mom said, "Awe Mom, do I have to go to school today? It is such a beautiful day. We could play at the beach!"

Warren Jr. was standing by the sink watching "his Mom". She really was a beautiful, athletic women. If his dad could not be with his Mom, Emily, then he was glad he could be with Becky. Under the circumstances it was a good match. It hurt his heart and soul that his Dad did not remember his Mom and that he was their son.

Warren Jr. himself, was having an increasing heaviness and ominous dread that something awful was about to happen. It just started about a month ago. He could not shake the feeling. He had called Sara several times and she assured him there was no apparent cause for alarm. He also called Grandma Flata and told her of his fears. However, his response from Grand Ma Flata was that everything was okay.

It took several years of being called Grandma before she had come to love it. All ten of the Andrian Hybrid children called her grandma, including the offspring of those whose parents came from the Intergalactic Carriers.

The original ten young children had been designed by Flata using Andrian and Human genes to help elevate Human intelligence. They were then inserted into Human repositors and raised as part of a family, with the Mother and Father being no less the wiser. Their insertion into the Human population was to help resolve environmental issues but had subsequently been kidnapped and held captive by the Andrian traitor Zelegark. Their exploratory adventures as to whom and what they were had been intense.

Retired New York City Homicide Detective Gary Jessop, and retired Los Angeles Homicide Detective Carol Reese met up at the University of Physics and Polymer Sciences having respectively retired from big city problems. Both had sought refuge to heal in the small, lazy, University town. The University was a medium sized school in the sleepy hamlet town in Blaizon Hills. After all, what could go wrong with a bunch of nerdy kids?

Their superior investigative skills had been instrumental in tracking down Emily Smith who had been kidnapped by the Andrian, Blain, to protect her from the Traitor Zelegark. And, their discretionary methods of investigation had not gone unnoticed by Space Intelligence. Thus because of their skills and discretionary judgement they exhibited it led them to being recruited by Space Intelligence as Investigators.

As Detectives Jessop and Reese had discussed the offer extended by Space Intelligence, they both decided it would be a different avenue of investigation. Like Jessop said, "Why not Carol, neither one of us have ever hunted aliens?" Thus, their efforts had born fruit in the form of finding and freeing ten young children from a sham Mental Hospital ran by Zelegark. He had killed their parents and imprisoned the children and was awaiting execution orders from his co-conspirators.

Warren Jr., whom the family called Junior, said, "Mom, that is really a good idea. Why do you not take the day off and spend some really good mother-daughter time with Lilly? Take some pictures, you know how fast she is growing up."

Becky thought for a minute and then remembered her night terrors.

"You know Junior, I think you are right. Lilly and I will have a Mother-Daughter day, we will go to the beach. Would you like to come along?"

Lilly laughed in delight. She loved spending time with her mother and knew how exciting it would be to go to the beach.

"No thanks Mom, I have some things I have to do on a school assignment. But thank you for the invite."

Warren Junior could read her thoughts and he knew what her night terrors were about. They were the same fears he was having, only he was awake. He knew that soon she would remember everything as her memories were too strong to be suppressed much longer. He would probably have to tell her soon. He would talk to Sara. She would know best what to do.

CHAPTER 13
WARREN JR.'S HEART

Warren Jr. left for school. At seventeen he was average age for a boy in high school, a senior at that. It did not help him much in the dating game because he was a loner and he did not have time to think about girls anyway. Warren Jr. could easily have been in a Masters or Doctorates level of study at a university. Sara told him he would be of more service in identifying exceptional young students that would be candidates for evacuation should that become necessary. It was such a heavy responsibility. There was no joy in deciding basically who would live and who would die should it come to a mass evacuation. His only solace was in knowing that all the student's DNA had been taken and was stored in an Andrian data bank. That way in some distant future and some faraway place each of them would live on, neither would have knowledge of the other. Flata was in charge of that phase of the program.

Warren Jr. decided to take a short drive thru the forest where he knew there was a small pond. He needed time to think. He parked between two giant spruce trees. Exiting his car, he padded his way thru the foliage to the pond. Exiting the foliage into the meadow, Warren Jr. observed a young girl twirling and dancing on the grass. She was wearing a long, light colored dress that seemingly floated around her body. It was pastel with light blues and pink blending together. The dress brought to mind the pastel colors on the Intergalactic Carrier as they blended together on the wall in some of the living areas. Warren Jr. smiled at the memory, he had forgotten about the experience, almost.

The young girl appeared to be about fifteen years of age. He knew almost everyone in the area and he had never seen her before. The girl raised her arms and her face toward the sun with her eyes closed, her long blond hair blowing into the wind. She was beautiful. Her arms were pale and her body was reed thin, her bare feet was splayed in the grass.

She intoned, "Oh thank you God for this beautiful day!"

The girl fell back on the ground and lay there enjoying the moment of peace and tranquility. She seemed to sense another presence and lifting herself on her elbow she turned toward Warren Jr. Upon seeing him her face colored beet red and she jumped up ready to run.

Warren without thinking exclaimed loudly, "Please, do not go. I did not mean to impose on you. I know of this spot and I just needed some time to think."

The girl stopped and looked directly at him into his eyes. She was not afraid; his sudden appearance had just startled her.

Warren Jr. was mesmerized by the palest blue eyes he had ever seen. She was not wearing makeup of any kind, yet her lips were full and pink. Warren Jr.'s heart skipped a beat. Reading her mind, he could sense that she was also drawn to him. He could also feel a sense of deep despair. Almost like defeat. The exuberance she was feeling earlier slowly ebbed from her spirit.

"My name is Warren Jr. I go to the local high school." Then adding sheepishly, "I am a senior".

"Why would I say that? It sounds so corny, like I am tooting my own horn or something. Why would I care what this girl thought of me?"

"Well my name is Alice. I flunked the ninth grade."

The girl named Alice just stood there looking at him with a somewhat mischievous smile on her face.

"I know almost everyone around here and I have never seen you before, and why on earth would you flunk the ninth grade?"

Alice replied, "It is sort of complicated."

Warren Jr. responded, "Well I can understand complicated, that is if you are willing to tell me." Warren understood secrets and complications and knew full well he could not tell Alice everything about himself even though for some strange reason he wanted too. What was that all about?

Remembering his manners, Warren Jr. said, "I am sorry, I did not mean to pry. It is just that you are...so beautiful and full of life, and I am so drawn to you for some strange reason and I have never felt this way about a girl before", with the last part of his declaration mumbled. It was his turn to turn beet red realizing what he had said.

Alice gave a wistful smile. "I wish I were full of life, and yes, it is really heartwarming that you find me attractive. But that is not to be. You see, I am terminally ill. Although it was nice to hear you say you think I am beautiful. I have a brain tumor and my time is limited."

Laughing, Alice said, "To bad you are not in the seventh grade, maybe we could play dolls together!"

Warren Jr. did not know when one would play dolls together as he had never been in the seventh grade. But at the mention of dolls, Warren Jr. remembered the little cowboy doll his mom Emily had made him when he was on the Carrier, it seemed like so long ago. This time it was he who had the wistful look in his eye.

Alice seeing this, changed the subject and said, "I live with my Grandmother. She has a house about a mile from here. My Mom and Dad died in an automobile crash when I was four, so, my Grandmother raised me. My Grandfather died a long time before I came along.

Warren Jr. responded, "Well, my Mom is in the military on a long deployment. I have not seen her since I was seven. I really do not know if she is alive or dead, although I think The Cosmic Spirit would let me know if she were dead. My Dad finally remarried and now I call Becky, "Mom". I also have a little sister named, Lilly, she is eight.

Alice looked at Warren Jr. very solemnly and said, "That is complicated".

If his Mother taught him anything, it was that things happened for a reason. Meeting Alice was no accident. Warren Jr. said, "Do you believe in providence? I do, my whole family lives or dies by it. That is how we survive. I believe we were destined to meet and it was arranged by the Great Cosmic Spirit. What comes about after that is determined by how we act upon the opportunities provided by the Cosmic Spirit."

"I have never heard of, "The Great Cosmic Spirit". Alice assumed it was just another name for God. Alice had accepted her fate two years ago and had since made her peace with God. Meeting this boy named Warren Jr. was not going to change the outcome of her approaching death, providence or not.

"What are you doing today?", Warren Jr. suddenly asked.

"I would like for you to meet my Grandmother".

Alice looked at Warren Jr. a minute then said, "Okay, but then you have to come and meet my Grandmother".

With the meeting of the Grandmothers settled, Alice accompanied Warren Jr. off thru the woods to his car then he started driving to Emilie's.

"Are you not a little young to be driving"? Queried Alice.

CHAPTER 14
TRANSCENDENCE

Emily slowly showered and lathered her hair to a large puffy snowball. Taking her time rinsing off, Emily was aware she used a week's allotment of water. Thinking to herself, "I doubt if I will need any water when I have become "One" with the female bio mechanical Entity within the Carrier".

Emily exited the shower and saw Blain standing in the passageway waiting for her. Before he could say anything, Emily said, "Blain, I know you have a lot of questions and I understand that. But you know as well as I that I do not have any answers. I do not know where this immersion of my Spirit Being with the Entities Spirit Being will take us. It may be possible for me to come back to you whole and sound. Perhaps there will be a matrix copy of me stored somewhere aboard the ship in one of the computers or something. All I know is that this is something I have to do. At any rate, my DNA is stored here and perhaps I can be reincorporated at another time in another place."

Smiling, then Emily said, "You can make a whole bunch of Emilie's and plant us all over the Universe".

Emily took Blain's hand and pulled him into their sleeping quarters. They had been so busy since arriving and meeting with the different captains of the intergalactic carriers that they did not have any time for themselves. Emily decided to have one last selfish time with her husband. She knew her time as a corporal being was short. They made love, at first feverishly, then gently, falling asleep in one another's arms.

Blain woke up dreamily feeling sated and at peace, more so than he had in a log time. He reached over to put his arms around Emily and pull her close, smell her hair and kiss her lips. His arms fell on an empty space.

Blain had never cried in his life. He really did not know what tears were other than an affliction suffered by humans. But at the realization that Emily was truly gone, his heart wrenched, his vision blurred and he fell to his knees with a loud animal like wail coming from his lips. Tears poured from his eyes in never ending rivulets. All the Andrian inbred self-control for a thousand generations released in a flood of anguished pain. And also, for a first, a prayer from his heart passed his lips as he begged the Cosmic Spirit to return Emily to him.

CHAPTER 15
A SHARED HEART

Warren Jr. drove to Emily's place which was about thirty miles away. Neither he nor Alice spoke. Alice was thinking what a strange boy he was.

"He was obviously smart otherwise he would not already be a senior in high school. He did not appear to be to adept around girls as he flustered easily and was unsure how to present his best foot forward, as was noted in his attempt to exhibit his superior intellectual abilities. He was sweet, kind and obviously infatuated with me. His declaration of being in the twelfth grade was a masked attempt to be accepted by me."

Whatever his feelings were for her she was comfortable with him. She had never told anyone else she was going to die. "Why did I tell him?" Alice moved away from the window and scooted next to Warren Jr. Just being next to him brought a sense of being normal. And by telling him she was going to die relieved a heavy burden she did not realize she was carrying.

Warren on the other hand, was in turmoil. He did not understand his feelings for Alice. How could he possibly be so taken aback so quickly? It was like magic except he did not believe in magic. The only thing he knew is that this girl must not die. But again, on the other hand, she had no self-redeeming value. She was already sick.

Without intervention she was going to die and relatively soon. He had entered her mind and he confirmed she had a malignant tumor and she absolutely had little to no math skills. In an Andrian society they were assuredly necessary as the air they breathed. If she were the standard of acceptance, they would all surely die. How could he possibly justify saving her having excluded an innumerable number of more worthy candidates to a certain horrible death?

Warren Jr's heart became heavy. For the first time in his life he questioned what he was planning on doing even though he did not allow the thought to formulate in his mind. He would call Sara and council with her. That too would be a first.

Sara watched the car come up the drive. She was intrigued as to what exactly Warren Jr. wanted. It obviously was very important as he had never called her before wanting to talk about something personal.

Flata, sitting next to Sara said, "Is that a girl sitting next to Warren Jr.? Well wouldn't you know it. It is always about a girl!"

Flata smiled broadly. The ability for Flata to smile was definitely a new dimension to her ingrained, austere character. And she so loved the role of being a grandmother and having all the children call her grandmother.

The two women stood as the couple got out of the car and proceeded up the porch stairs. Reading their minds, they knew instantly what Warren Jr. wanted. Sara smiled at Warren Jr.'s love for the girl. Sara gave him a long embrace and said, "I love you so much little brother".

Alice looked at Warren Jr. in surprise, as she remembered he had said he only had a little sister and her name was Lilly.

Warren Jr., reading Alice's mind, looked at Alice and said, "It is complicated, you will soon understand."

Sara took Alice in her arms and gave her a hug. "It is so nice to meet you. Warren Jr. never steppes out of the parameters which he is assigned and for him to do so means that you are very important to him. And if you are important to him you are of the utmost importance to us."

Alice did not know what to say. For her to say Warren Jr. stepped out of his parameters sounded strange. It was just an odd thing to say. And yes, it went along with her odd fashion sense. The black jump suit looked military but not like any military uniform she had ever seen. Then she was somewhat startled to notice the four, armed soldiers around their perimeter. How did they get there? She had not seen them before when they walked up the stairs.

Sara said, "Alice, is it? Please have a seat. It is such a surprise to meet you. As I said, Warren Jr. never steppes outside of the established protocols and for him to bring someone here is unprecedented. So, little brother. why have you not told us of this lovely young lady before now?"

Warren spoke out loud for Alice's sake and replied, "I just met her today. I do not understand it, but I think I am in love with her and I do not want anything bad to happen to her. I do not want to be without her, wherever we may be."

Alice looked at Warren Jr. in amazement. "But you just met me. The only thing you know about me is that I am going to die and very soon!"

Warren Jr. replied, "But Alice that is not true. I know your heart is pure, your spirit is at peace with the Cosmic Spirit. You know you are going to die thru no fault of your own and yet you are not bitter. Your primary worry is for your grandmother and how she will cope without you as you are her only living relative. You took a chance with me and told me of your impending death not knowing what my response would be. Well my response is this, I love you Alice, and I want to spend the rest of my life with you."

Tears came to Alice's eyes. "How can that possibly be. My life is nothing if not short. How could we even think such a thing, I am only fourteen. What an awful burden for you carry". Then she momentarily smiled and said, "Even if you are a senior in high school, you smarty pants!"

Sara and Flata burst out laughing and Sara said, "Warren Jr.! Has she got you pegged! You are a smarty pants!"

Warren Jr. agreed that he was indeed a smarty pants but quickly changed the subject, looked at Flata and said, "Grand Mother Flata, can you help Alice?"

To Alice he said, "My Grand Mother is a healer and can work miracles. I know she can help you. If anyone can heal you it will be her."

Alice bit her lower lip and tears slid down her cheeks.

Alice turned and faced Warren Jr. and placed her hand on his leg. "Warren, I have been to some of the best doctors in the state. They all agree that the tumor has increased in size and is becoming more aggressive daily. They were just being kind to me by saying I had two more years to live. I know I only have a few months. If I do not take my medicine daily, I get so ill I cannot stand up. I am afraid to lay down because I may not ever get up again."

Flata looked at the young girl. She had entered the young girls mind and knew she was deathly ill. Actually, should not immediate intervention occur, she would be dead within weeks.

"My dear, why do you not let me examine you. It will not take long. And, like Warren Jr. said, miracles can happen. I think we should start with a cup of warm tea."

Saying this Flata got up and went into the house. She called for a transport and put a strong relaxer into Alice's tea to put Alice asleep. Alice drank her tea, became drowsy and placed her head on Warren Jr.'s shoulder and was soon fast asleep. The transport came and Alice was loaded into the transport and Flata accompanied it to the base hospital deep in the mountain leaving Sara and Warren Jr. alone on the porch.

Sara said, "What of the grandmother? I doubt that Alice will leave her behind should it come to an evacuation."

Warren thought for a moment, then said, "I am sure that she will want what is best for Alice. I will tell her the truth, give her a potent so when the time comes, she will not suffer. Alice will understand."

"And Sara, about my dreams, they are becoming more intense. And, Becky is having them too. I believe she must be told the truth soon or she will learn the truth on her own. I think you and I should tell her to make it easier on her."

Sara replied, "I too have been having dreams and wake up in a sweat. Since we are all having them it must mean something. Perhaps our time is short. We should consider increasing the rate of Ark launches immediately. We have not heard anything from the fleet since your Mother left. We are going to be very busy. In the meantime, let's go visit Alice's grandmother."

CHAPTER 16

A Grand Mother's Solemn Joy

Both Sara and Warren Jr. believed the most direct approach was the only way to inform Alice's Grandmother of the coming events, therefore, they landed their saucer on her front lawn. Upon exiting the saucer, they saw her sipping tea or coffee on her front porch. She was observing them like it was an everyday occurrence, although somewhat apprehensive.

When they got to the porch Sara said, "Mrs. Wayne, please forgive us for such an unorthodox entry but we are on a time schedule and we need to discuss some matters that pertain to your Granddaughter, Alice."

At the mention of Alice, Mrs. Wayne's alarm spiked.

"Mrs. Wayne, please do not be alarmed. Alice is fine. In fact, as we speak, she is being healed of her brain tumor. May we join you for tea?"

Mrs. Wayne got up and retrieved two additional cups from the cupboard and poured tea for them both.

Mrs. Wayne gave a short laugh and said, "When I got up this morning, I imagined many different things that might happen today but you certainly, was not one of them."

Sara and Warren Jr. laughed with Sara saying, "I

imagine not".

Sara said, "My name is Sara Sears and this young man," indicating Warren Jr., is my little brother. Your granddaughter Alice and Warren Jr. met earlier this morning. They are both enamored with one another. And as I said, Alice is being tended to by an Andrian geneticist doctor name Flata. Flata is my surrogate mom and Warren Jr's grandmother.

Sara and Warren spent the next two hours providing an abbreviated synopsis of their life up to this moment in time, leaving out the moment of truth where her granddaughter was going to have to leave her behind to an all but certain death.

Mrs. Wayne was silent for several minutes as she studied the two people in front of her. Mrs. Wayne had lived a long time and if she was aware of anything, she knew these two people did not drop by in their flying saucer just to chat about her granddaughters love interest. The woman was obviously in some kind of military as she exhibited several subtle scars. The young man was by all appearances like any other young man even though he wore the same kind of jump suit.

Mrs. Wayne asked, "Is the Earth in some kind of trouble? And, are you going to take as many people with you as you can? And of course, they would have to be young, like Alice, to qualify for the trip."

Warren Jr. said, "You are correct in several aspects of your deduction with the exception that Alice would be included because she is young. Alice is included because I love her and she loves me. On her own she would not qualify. She has no math or science skills what so ever. So many others more worthy of life have been excluded because the requirements are so stringent. A space faring society requires mathematical and science skills above all others if it is to survive the rigors of space."

"The Andrians forefathers have been travelling between the galaxies before our ancestors climbed out of the trees. Now we are adding homo sapiens to the mix and hopefully we can modify some of their ingrained social customs. We will be taking with us DNA patterns of every living human being upon the earth including yours.

And yes, the scourge which we are all facing is not a Hollywood fixation of a scary movie. We are fighting for our very existence. My Mother is the Co-Commander of the Andrian Battle Fleet somewhere past the Andromeda Galaxy. At this moment in time I do not know if she is alive or dead. However, I am sure the Great Cosmic Spirit would allow us to know if her fate was that of death. I do not feel that thus I have hope she is still alive. I have not seen her since she left ten years ago when I was seven.

The lifeform which we are fighting is not carbon based as we are. It is believed by many scientists, to have come from another dimension due to a rent in the space time continuum. There does not appear to be any other explanation. They absolutely kill every living thing on a planet and leave it drenched in highly caustic acid. Once they arrive, no one escapes.

However, there are two exceptions. A specie of mermaids and a specie of Neanderthals were saved by my

TARGET EARTH

Mom and the bio-mechanical entity within her space craft. It is believed that our species is the only one to stand against them successfully and thus their hatred for us propels them toward earth. The Andrian and Earth military commands working together can slow them down but their arrival is inevitable. Their numbers are too great and we cannot generate enough black holes to swallow them all.

After this long expository of the Human-Andrian confrontation with the other dimensional life form Warren Jr. became quiet. He believed he covered the salient points quiet well. Mrs. Wayne was the only person in the whole world, other than military and pertinent scientist to receive such a briefing.

Mrs. Wayne asked, "Will I be alive when they arrive?"

Sara handed a blue vial of liquid to Mrs. Wane and said, "Should that happen, drink this. It is quick and painless, just like dropping off quickly to sleep".

Mrs. Wayne took the vial and asked if she would see Alice again.

Warren Jr. responded, "Yes, come with us now and stay as long as necessary."

Mrs. Wayne got up and said, "Let me get my coat and my purse. I see no necessity to lock up. And just before she went out the door, she picked up an old, used, black guitar case that contained Alice's guitar.

CHAPTER 17
SECOND CHANCE

Alice groggily stretched her arms and yawned a long satisfying yawn. She felt so good and rested. Nor did she feel the subtle pressure in her head which she had become so accustomed too. Looking around Alice found herself in a rustic bedroom with picture windows overlooking the bay. She could hear the muffled sound of talking coming from another part of the house. She could even hear her grandmother laughing.

Looking down she saw she was clothed in a short sleeved, bright, multi colored shift and was wearing soft cloth slippers. As she walked toward the door, she passed a full, length mirror and was startled to see her image. She looked so healthy. She was no longer pale and her hair was glossy and had the rich luster again as it was before the cancer treatment. She looked closely and could not see any indication that she had had an operation.

"Well maybe she could not help me after all, even though I look better and feel better. At least there was that", thought Alice.

Alice continued out the door and down the stairs into the living area. Alice observed her grandmother sitting in a chair with a drink in her hand. Her legs were casually crossed and she looked…so at ease. There were no worry wrinkles around her eyes or down her cheeks. And she had such a pretty smile.

Alice then saw Warren Jr. walking toward her. He was smiling and said, "Alice, you look beautiful!"

Alice heard his voice but she did not see his lips move. She was confused. Again, Warren Jr. spoke to her saying, "How do you feel Alice? I told you my grandmother could heal you of the brain tumor. Not only that, she enhanced your linguistic skills so you can hear and speak telepathically! And that is only the beginning! Cool, huh!"

Again, Alice heard Warren Jr. speak and then observed it was in her head and not with her ears as his lips did not move.

Flustered, Alice exclaimed, "How is that possible?"

Warren Jr. reached out his hand and escorted Alice into the room. The room was crowded with several young people their age. The two older women whom she had met earlier were visiting with her grandmother. They stopped conversing and acknowledged Alice's presence.

Alice's grandmother got up from her chair and ran and pulled Alice into her arms exclaiming, "God has answered my prayers for you Alice, in the most profound and amazing way! You have been cured of your brain cancer! And not only that but your brain has been awakened and enhanced so you will have access to a greater portion of your brain than you had before the operation. Now you can actually do the math in your checkbook!"

Everyone laughed.

The older woman whom she had heard referred to as Flata came over to her and took both her hands and said,

"Look at me child. I want to see how you feel."

Flata looked closely into Alice's eyes and listened to her thought processes. She entered her mind slowly and she could not sense any remaining malignant tumors. She was satisfied that she had done such a good job because in truth the girl was on the verge of dying and actually had only weeks to live.

Without verbally speaking to Alice, she said, "I found the area of your brain that enable you to play your instrument to be highly developed while the area of your brain that allows for mathematical solving of problems to be almost non-existent. Poor girl, how have you managed to survive!"

Everyone in the room were quietly listening as Flata had allowed the communication to be communal and Flata's comment about Alice surviving with little to no mathematical skills was for Flata a joke because all the Andrians knew that humans were all inept in and lacking such abilities. All the children laughed.

Warren Jr. brought Alice a small plate of food and a cool glass of water and encouraged her to eat and drink. Indeed, Alice realized she was famished and ate heartily while the rest of the group quietly conversed. When she had eaten every crumb on her plate Alice sat back and sighed. "That was so good. I have not eaten that much since I do not know when!"

Warren Jr. then explained to Alice who he was and the circumstances which brought them all to their current predicament. She was very quiet as she listened to the litany of circumstances that portended the end of human life on the planet earth. Tears slid down her cheeks and she tightly held her grandmother's hand. Her feelings and emotions were in a state of chaos. Here she had just been given a new lease on life with the cure of her cancer and her new found love for Warren Jr. and the joy in her heart had been overwhelming. And then, in the next breath she learns that everything she knew and loved was in all probability going to be destroyed by some malignant nemesis from outer space.

Alice's grandmother took Alice in her arms as Alice cried tears of despair. The tears were many and her sobs were deep and shook Alice to her very core. But they were healing tears as they had been held back for years as Alice bravely faced her trials and tribulations of her ever-growing cancer. That burden having now been lifted left her emotions bare and with the revelations of things yet to come, almost overwhelmed her.

All the young people in the room gathered around Alice and placed their hands on her and softly infused her with their strength and their love. They understood how enlightenment and knowledge could be a heavy burden. And, under the circumstances, with ignorance being bliss and knowledge being enlightenment, it did not change the fact that they could soon all die a quick and gruesome death.

CHAPTER 18
THANK YOU FOR LOVING ME

Becky was busy in the kitchen when she saw Sara and Warren Jr. drive up in their car. She had just put cookies in the oven for Lilly and was excited to see Sara. She had not seen her for at least two months. When Sara came around, she usually tried to make sure Warren was at work because for some strange reason Warren would become agitated and he really did not like her.

Sara and Becky gave one another a long hug exclaiming their love for one another. Warren Jr. quietly stood by the side watching somewhat apprehensively as he and Sara decided that he was the one that should tell Becky the circumstances of his and her, Becky's, relationship. Warren Jr. was thinking that nothing in his young life had ever been simple. He had, had "fun". Warren had taken him sailing several times and now he was a somewhat accomplished sailor. But for the most part he was a loner. His duties had precluded him from making close friends. His friends consisted of family. He made it a point to visit with Orion and Perilain often. They would discuss their individual duties and each despaired over the choices they were required to make.

After Sara and Becky finished their greetings, Becky

got some cold drinks and they sat outside in the shade of a large oak tree. The oak had to be over one hundred years old and had limbs spanning at least as many feet as it was years old. Warren Jr. did not know how to start the conversation out so he opted with his fortunate meeting of Alice.

"Mom, good news first! I met a girl. Her name is Alice and she is so beautiful. I cannot wait for you to meet her! I am going to marry her!"

The part about marriage shocked not only Becky but Warren Jr. too. He had not quiet cleared in his mind the direction their relationship was going to take. Of course, he knew they would eventually be together as boyfriend and girlfriend but the word marriage had not been formulated within his mind.

Becky was taken aback. "Marriage! What are you talking about? Who is this Alice? How come you never brought her home? I mean come on Warren. You have never even been with a girl in your entire life! I mean it is not like you to have been keeping secrets from me. You have always been the perfect son. I do not think you have ever lied to me, have you?"

At this point Sara interjected, "Well there is more. Now is the time Warren. Tell her." Sara was of course referring to the dreams and relationships.

Becky was already somewhat angry and her anger went from being aggravatingly miffed at Warren Jr. for not informing her about him having a girlfriend to lava hot having jumped to the wrong conclusion.

Becky Literally screamed, "No! No! You do not, do

not dare tell me she is pregnant! How could you?"

Warren Jr's face turned beet red. He felt like the well laid plans he had formulated had just been totally destroyed. He assumed that Alice would be a light subject and he wanted to introduce Becky to her before he told her the hard stuff. So much for well laid plans.

Sara felt sorry for Warren Jr. because she believed this meeting was hard enough without interjecting false assumptions into the mix.

Sara said, "Becky, there is more and it is not about Alice being or not being pregnant. She is not pregnant. I wish by the stars that was all there is to it. It is much more serious than that. I believe we have all been having dreams. Difficult dreams."

Warren Jr. said," Mom, I have been having them too, just like you, and Sara, also. I hear you at night when you are deep asleep and you have to fight to wake up because of the terror they cause you. The dreams are so intense you have difficulty breathing and when you finally wake up you are choking back screams. Therefore, it is time to reveal to you another truth. We, Sara and I, believe it would be best for you to learn this truth from us."

Warren Jr. just did not know any other way to say what he had to say other than directly without any equivocation. Looking around he made sure Lilly was playing elsewhere. She was.

Becky was looking at Warren Jr. like he was toying with her but she knew he was not because he looked so sincere and…mature. "What could he possibly have to say?" thought Becky.

"Mom, Becky, I am not your biological son. However, you are just as much my Mother as Emily. We are going to restore your memories so you will understand. It is so important that we work together because we believe that possibly my mom, Emily, is trying to contact us and provide critical information thru dreams."

Becky just sat there looking at them as if they were crazy. "Of course, you are my son, silly! I should know after all I went thru, all the pain of the birth!"

Sara and Warren Jr. stood and moved to each side of Becky. They placed their hands on the sides of her head, similar to but not the same as, a church blessing, and both Becky and Warren Jr. used mental telepathy instilling a prearranged string of code words which would restore Becky's memory.

Becky stood up and took Warren Jr. in her arms and with tears streaming down her face she said, "I love you so much. I am so proud of you. You are, and always will be, my son."

Warren Jr. was crying also and he hugged his "mom" saying, "I am so blessed to have you as a Mom. The times and circumstances are so hard."

Sara took charge since the sensitive and difficult portion of the conversation had been broached.

Sara said, "I have been given the assignment by Emily that I am personally responsible for all of our families. When and if we evacuate, you need to know we are already assigned to the same carrier. As for Warren, he will never know until he wakes up in space. A fleet of carriers have already been built and the construction is still continuing. Selections are being made as to whom to evacuate. There are not enough ships to evacuate everyone on the planet. We can evacuate only approximately five million people. And that is predicated on having enough time to do so. That is why our dreams are so important. It may be that Emily is trying to warn us. We must listen our dreams and try to remember what they are about. We will start meeting every morning to start evaluating our dreams and compare should there be any similarities. Since all our dreams are so intense, we feel like our time is short. We have decided to go ahead and launch the first Inter-Galactic Arc as soon as possible. We have candidates being loaded as we speak.

Becky thought for a minute then she said, "How are candidates selected and who makes the decision about who gets to go and who is left behind?"

Sara said, "There is a team of experts that research and evaluate which individuals will go. Warren Jr. is one of the individuals that selects the candidates and help make that decision.

Becky drew in her breath sharply and let out a clipped cry. Looking at Warren Jr., she finally understood the deep sorrowful reflection in his eyes.

CHAPTER 19
CREATION'S MISTY REALM

Emily could feel Blain next to her and listened to his breathing. It was even, deep, and contented. She slowly rose to a sitting position and leaned over and kissed him on the lips one last time. He did not stir. Rising out of bed she went to the shower and again took a long, leisurely, hot shower. She justified this by knowing that in all probability it would be her last. She had no idea what kind of self-indulgent, personal pleasures awaited her in the mystic realm in which she was going to reside with the Entity, but she believed them to be few if any.

Emily toweled off and combed her hair and tied it back into a ponytail. She put on her uniform but opted not to take a weapon. She did not think a mystical spirit would have need of a laser blaster. Emily quietly padded out of the sleeping quarters to the passageway. Two soldiers assigned for her protection immediately stood at attention and saluted. She returned a crisp salute in the proper and correct manner. She was always humbled by the many men and women that were willing to follow her to their deaths if she so ordered. The weight of leadership always weighed heavily on her spirit. She strived to make the right decisions.

As Emily rounded a corner, she found Sasha waiting for her having been informed by Emily's security detail that she was on the move. Both women embraced in a silent melding of spirit. Both women cried a few tears and after a long sweet embrace, they parted. Sasha accompanied Emily to where ever Emily was going as she had no knowledge of the destination. Neither woman spoke as communal silence is the most sublime communication of those whose loving spirits are in tune. Loved ones need not talk.

Emily proceeded to the area in the Intergalactic Carrier that she had been directed to go to by the Entity. The location was in the bowels of the Carrier close to the laser generators. Before opening the hatch, Emily hugged both members of her security detail and kissed Sasha one last time.

"After I leave, go to our bed and be with Blain. Love him for the both of us!"

Then, without another word to Sasha, verbal or otherwise, Emily opened the hatch and went into the chamber. As Emily closed the hatch behind her, she instructed her security escort team that they should stand by for one hour, and, if she did not come out, they were to return to her quarters and stand by for Blain and Sasha.

Emily went and stood in the middle of the chamber in a muted red light that emanated from the bulkhead, waiting.

"Welcome my love." The soft feminine voice melodiously reverberated thru the chamber.

Emily responded, "If we are going to do this, if you can do this, then lets' proceed."

The Entity said, "Always the commander. You will not feel any pain. And, I honestly do not know if you can return to your corporeal body. With your permission, we shall proceed. You will be atomized down to your molecular structure. You will be as you were in your dreams feeling every nuance of creation interacting with your atoms. We will begin now."

Emily said a silent prayer that risking her life in this manner would not be in vain but she would do anything to save the lives of her loved ones. The red light in the room began to rotate increasing in intensity. There was a piercing hum that increased in decibels. Emily did not feel any pain but she could feel an immense pressure. She began to feel light headed. All feeling left her feet and legs then her arms. Her torso became expansive. She could see her lower body begin to drift away in tiny particles. The particles broke down farther still until they were no longer visible to her. She felt her face pulling away and she had a moment of intense regret but it was for only a second. Then she passed out losing consciousness and falling into a deep well of darkness.

"Emily! Emily! Welcome my love! I have longed for this moment for an eternity! Now that we are one, we can defeat the menace that is destroying our universe. I am gathering our quarks so we may travel vast distances quickly and learn what dimension this life form came from."

Emily slowly became cognizant with her mind

seemingly divided into many parts. One part of her mind was focused on the dark matter drive within the cryogenics chamber of the Intergalactic Carrier. Another part of mind could see every crew member of the ship and knew exactly what they were doing. Yet another section of her mind was intermingling within the ship of the acid-based lifeforms. Then to her amazement she could see her family on the earth and observe the things they were doing. They seemed to be moving so slow in their progress of building the Intergalactic Arks for the evacuation of select individuals. They needed to hurry! The enemy had scattered thru out the void and some was approaching their Milky Way Galaxy.

The Entity of which she was now a part of spoke to yet another level of her consciousness and directed her to join her with a visit to a different dimension to ascertain if they could lure the enemy there to lock them in a time warp.

The first dimension to which they traveled was different from anything Emily could have ever imagined. There were mountains of atoms which seemed to pass by almost at the speed of light. There were voids between the mountains where vast fields of muons were lined up in orderly rows as if waiting to be called upon to serve some purpose and function. Quarks formed vertical walls on each side of the muons.

Sometime when a mountain of atoms whizzed by chains of muons would join the mountain which would then become an explosion of intermingling activity. There was no up or down, there was just a presence of quarks that would appear and disappear as they traveled in what appeared to be a chaotic band of light.

The Entity and Emily traveled thru several dimensions, some had lifeforms with the same molecular structure as themselves but in and of itself the combinations of genetic structure was not recognizable. They were living entities unto themselves. There was no way they could lead and abandon the acid-based life forms in these dimensions.

"Emily my love. I believe that we must go into a time warp and lead the enemy into not only a different dimension but a different universe in time. We need to go to as near the beginning of all things as possible. Also, I know you believe in a higher power that is even greater than us. If at all possible, you should make contact with this power and seek assistance. Since I am a bio mechanical construct, I do not believe they would heed me."

Emily replied, "This is true. We need to return to the ship and try and commune with the Cosmic Power."

When the Entity and Emily returned to the ship the ships chronometer indicated they had been gone for five years. The other sections of Emily's mind had continued working on the problems and challenges the acid-based enemy presented.

Another section of Emily's mind had been on the planet earth constantly trying to contact her family members thru dreams to admonish them to work faster. It amazed her that they were so dull of hearing. Emily saw the men attack Hanlee and she saw the young girl standing on the bank downstream. She focused her energy on the young girl and caused her to look up in time to see Hanlee floating in the water nearby. She found it interesting that she could not affect the outcome of human intentions and actions to do evil as they had their free agency to do as they wished. However, she could influence the young girl to look up and see Hanlee floating in the water.

Emily knew that she could affect behavior when she was on the earth, she could enter one's mind and influence behavior by directing an individual to turn right or left. She could also wipe an individual's mind of memories and plant other false memories. However, she could not prevent men from doing their evil acts if it was in their heart to do so. Emily realized that free agency reigned supreme on the earth and the spiritual realm as well.

Emily knew an attack on the earth was imminent thus she plagued Sara's, Warren Jr's and Becky's dreams about the coming events. Strange as it seemed to her Becky was the most receptive to her intrusions. But at last Sara and Warren Jr. both became cognizant of the fact that perhaps their dreams were indicative that she was trying to warn them of the impending disaster. Thus, they set in motion the first evacuation plan.

Emily and the Entity had been fairly successful in leading the enemy away from the earth into a time warp that dumped them into a vast starless void. They repaired the rift between the human universe and the enemy's entry point into the same universe. Hopefully they would not see them again, However, a large contingent chose not to follow and the Intergalactic Fleet engaged them in battle time and time again. At least they were not the

TARGET EARTH

innumerable host they once were as their ranks were not replenished and their numbers were dwindling it looked like perhaps, they could win the battles. However, they ominously believed they could possibly lose the earth.

CHAPTER 20
MESSAGE FROM AFAR

The frivolity was interrupted with the slamming of the screen door and two older men in military attire came out and stood at attention in front of Sara and saluted. Sara stood at attention and returned the salute.

"At ease gentlemen".

Commander Taaker, the ranking Andrian officer on the planet advised, "A ship just arrived from the Andromeda galaxy. They have a communique to you from The Captain, "Your Eyes Only."

Alice did not see anything unusual about the tall slender officer but the other officer, Wow! Was he handsome? He was built with strong features of Muskular arms, neck and chest. His face had discernable scars should one care to look. He had ice blue eyes that seemed to peer into ones very soul. Alice felt like a deer caught in headlights when he looked her way, smiled, and nodded his head. He acted like he knew her.

At about that time Alice could feel Warren Jr. beginning to lean on her. Warren Jr.'s mouth went dry; his legs became wobbly. He did not notice that he was about to fall but Alice quickly held him up with her arms around his shoulders and her hips bracing his legs giving him support. The shock of suddenly receiving a communication from his Mother after all these years caught him completely by surprise.

Sara took the envelope and before walking away she went up to the other ruggedly, handsome, looking officer, reached up and kissed him on the cheek saying, "Hi Dad", and walked to the end of the porch away from everyone else and opened the communique.

"Earth Commander, Sara Sears. We have engaged the enemy numerous times killing untold millions of them. But to no avail. They replenish their ranks immediately. We have released numerous viruses and chemical matrixes into their mist with little to no effect. The only way to stop them is to send them back to their dimension which we are unable to do at this time. It appears their number one objective is to destroy the earth because we are the only specie that has been able to withstand them. We shall continue to fight them all the way across the void to our galaxy. However, short of a Cosmic Spirit intervention, there is no stopping them, we can only slow down the inevitable."

Then from Emily, "It is therefore to this end that I have made the decision to become One with the Entity within our star ship thus hoping to somehow give us the ability to lead the enemy back into their dimension or into a great void."

The communique continued again but this time written by the Intergalactic Carrier Commander per the instructions from Emily.

"Her council to you is twofold. Upon receiving this communique, you are to load and launch the first ark star ship immediately. You should not stop launching until you are prevented from doing so. They should go to the outer reaches of the farthest galaxy possible, no two starships going in same direction. There is to be no inter-communication from the star ship Arks once they leave the earth. Each ark is on it's on. All arks are to have duplicate DNA packets to insure the survival of all our species. It will be important to have Entity Tracers so if the situation permits everyone can be located at some far distant future."

"Secondly, Emily said she is going to become one with the Entity in our star ship. Hopefully this will enable us in some way to defeat the enemy or at least send it back to another dimension. I do not know what this will entail. I can tell you that previously the Entity has communicated with her thru dreams. Therefore, I beg you to listen to your dreams. Perhaps it is Emily trying to communicate with you thru them.

That was the end of the official communique. Also included was a personal letter written by Emily to her family members. The letter was dated with a star date which was translated by Commander Taaker as being nine years ago Earth time.

"Warren Jr., I am so sorry I had to leave you as a child. However, I know I left you in good hands. Becky was a good choice and she assured me she would love you as her own. Be strong, be brave and above all, be true to the Cosmic Spirit. There is no doubt in my mind that someday you will meet a lovely companion who will be your supportive soul mate. You will know who that person is when you meet her. I am not a seer but I believe she will be about three years younger than you, have long blonde hair and can play a mean guitar!"

Alice's jaw dropped in awe. "How could she know?", Exclaimed Alice!

"Persha, Blain sends his love. He is proud of how you assimilated and have three beautiful children. We all are proud of you."

"Perilain, your mother Sasha, and father Blain, sends you the stars that they name for you nightly. The beautiful flower for which you are named will bloom throughout eternity declaring their love for you."

"They, and I, know all of you children are involved in the selection process for evacuees and are aware of the tremendous burdens these decisions places on your spirits. We all wanted your childhood to be free of trauma but that was not to be. Another way to look at it is, you are where you are supposed to be and you are using the gifts you have been given by the Great Cosmic Spirit to help insure the survival of the Human, Andrian and other species. Your reward will be great and your names will forever reverently be spoken throughout the cosmos as long as our species live."

"Sara treat Warren with compassion; he will be difficult. I suggest that Becky feed him a good dinner and then sedate him and keep him sedated until you all are safe in space."

"And Sara, you and Jawane are a good match. The love you have for one another was slow and methodical in coming. See Sara, your part Andrian and did not even know it!"

"Hanlee, you will meet a man that will have a positive impact on your life, if you have not already done so. I feel as if he will call your spirit to him so you both may be eternally bonded.

"Muskula, my sister from the stars, you come with us and choose whom you will. We all must leave seed in the stars."

"Last but not least, Grand Mother Flata, I love you as my own as you truly are. Watch over all our children and family."

Flata sat stoically looking straight ahead. She had a steady stream of tears running down her face, her very first.

"Blain, Sasha, and myself are one. And we pray our Spirits may somehow infuse you with comfort, love, and heart. Listen to your dreams as it may be me visiting you.

"We have discovered that Saturn's spongy looking moon Hyperion is an interstellar space ship disguised as a moon. Blain and I discovered the entrance to the ship when we explored the moon on my first visit to the Inter Galactic Cruiser. You remember that, it was when those, naughty ole Gypsies kidnapped me and carried me away to be their cook!"

Everyone laughed at Emily's levity. That had been the cover story that homicide detectives Jessop and Reese concocted to hide Emily's abduction by aliens. Blain had taken her to save her life from the Andrian traitor Zelagark.

"Anyway, we discovered our enemy's dead lifeform in the crafts airlock. It appeared that the craft was designed for humanoid phenotypes. All the controls and seating areas would have been comfortable for us. Perhaps they were fleeing from their enemy as we are going to do ours. Of course, they were doing this about a million years before we came along. As to what happened to them is unknown; we think that perhaps the enemy trapped in the airlock was a scout as it was alone".

"We leave our love, hearts and dreams with you until we meet again. Love, Emily."

There were other communiques within the packet which were distributed throughout the fleet. Caleb had a letter from Selena for her son Shawn and for Caleb and their son Michael.

Upon Sara's finishing the verbal reading of the communication from Emily everyone was silent, each deep in their own thoughts. Warren Jr. had composed himself and believed more than ever his dreams came from his mom. And the sense of urgency was not a figment of his imagination. A great destruction was coming upon the earth. Everyone was thinking the same thing. It was time to begin launching the Arks.

Sara, reading every one's mind and each having the same thought, turned to Commander Taaker and said, "Initiate evacuations. We, as leaders and family, will go last. We do not have any more time."

Sara then walked up to her Father and said, "I love you Dad, this is what you have trained me for." After kissing him on the cheek she solemnly spoke a string of coded numbers into her communication device."

CHAPTER 21
FIRST TEARS OF DEPARTURE (TEN DAYS BEFORE INVASION)

Ricky accompanied Hanlee to the college after everyone tearfully said their good byes. Ricky had so many questions and even though he could read minds after Flata had enhanced his communication skills, he could only see a blank wall in Hanlee's mind. She did not wish to let him see what she was thinking.

Finally, she said, "Ricky, I am so fortunate that you came into my life. You literally brought me back from the dead. I love you and I hope you can continue to love me when we get on an Intergalactic Carrier. Our life styles are going to change. It is going to be very challenging for you and Tiffany. Of course, the only alternative is in all probability a very painful and gruesome death."

"This alien entity is believed to not be from our dimension. Our combined militaries have been unable to destroy them all. We have been told there are not enough black holes generated to receive them all. They want to destroy the earth because we have been the only species to successfully stand against them. That is why they are now bypassing all other worlds and coming directly to earth. Do you really understand the full ramifications of the scenario that is about to encompass the earth? At the time of the communication from Emily they were on the other side of the great void between our Galaxy and Canis Major Dwarf Galaxy."

"Literally billions of people will die here on the earth. And that is just one tear drop of pain compared to what has been experienced across our universe. An untold number of worlds in an unknown number of galaxies have been destroyed by this alien entity. Why the Cosmic Spirit would allow such a thing to happen is incomprehensible to us all."

"Our sole objective and purpose for the last ten years has been to locate individuals that exhibit superior mathematical and scientific skills that will give our species a chance to survive in space and start over on a new world somewhere in this galaxy or in another galaxy, maybe even a different universe."

"This has been a very heavy burden to carry. It requires me to reaffirm my Andrian roots and exclude my Human indoctrination. It is my duty, yet it hurts my soul and fills my dreams with dread. But it is now time to start the evacuation and migration. We must round up the chosen individuals and load them onto a Inter Galactic Carrier. From there they will be transported beyond Jupiter where the Arks are being manufactured and assembled. I am comforted to have you by my side during this most difficult time."

Ricky sat quietly by Hanlee's side thinking how the month had brought change to his and Tiffany's life. He was surprised that he found himself attracted to the slim young women beside him. And, to think she was not from earth. How would one ever know? Who would ever guess that a small family camping trip would impact them with such far reaching consequences? After Hanlee had approached him and kissed him on the porch, in front of everyone no less, they had not been separated. Their sensual time together had been exactly that, sensual. Hanlee moved in with him and Tiffany stayed with Alice. Although Alice had Warren Jr. for her new companion, they were constantly together as Warren Jr. had become a very busy young man.

Ricky sat on the back row of the class which was elevated and provided a clear view of Hanlee as she addressed her class. She had never missed class before and her week long absence from the students had them concerned. She was wearing light navy blue slacks with a blue blazer open at the front revealing a tight-fitting neck hugging, rose colored, blouse. The blue blazer had a spiral galaxy with seven stars across the top embraided above the left breast. The class was surprised to see Hanlee clothed in this manner as she always wore bright colored dresses. In fact, the outfit looked more like a uniform than her every day clothing.

Addressing the class, Hanlee said, "Good morning. Today I want your thoughts on a completely different scenario other than the discussion on atoms and the feasibility of fusion power for generating space and time travel. Let us suppose that the earth was in distress from an outside influence. This influence may be from a gamma ray burst from a distant galaxy, climate change drying up the water supply, the loss of earth's magnetic field due to the suns increase in its nuclear activity creating giant sunspots. Or perhaps even more dire, an alien threat for which we have no control over nor unable to defeat. It is important for you to understand that all the above listed scenarios I have listed is entirely possible. What should we do as a species to insure our survival?"

The class was perplexed at the turn of events in curriculum but enjoyed the new and fresh direction of the discussion and eagerly joined in offering many solutions for each and every event Hanlee had postulated. The thought of an alien invasion of course got the most attention, coming in first. Then with the possibility of the change in earth's magnetic field and perhaps flipping the earth one hundred and eighty degrees, coming in for a close second. After all, which was most plausible? Certainly not aliens, but it was the most interesting and entertaining.

The lecture hall was large and held two hundred students. Each of the students in this particular class was handpicked by Hanlee. The students were, in her opinion, mankind's best hope for survival. Unknown to them, today was going to be their last day of class. School was out, survival was in.

Addressing her class Hanlee said, "I have a pleasant surprise for you. We are going to take a field trip and the buses are out front. We will be back by four P.M., and I hope that will not be any problem for any of you. I came up with this idea when I was convalescing and I decided that learning should be more hands on and more fun than learning about a few atoms and quarks."

"As you obviously do not know, my brother and I was left alone when our mother and father was killed in a military action."

This was not true but it served a purpose.

"We were fortunate and blessed to have another family take us in. In effect, I have had several adult mother and father figures in my life, all which love me dearly. And as my mother and father before them, they too are in the military."

"I have observed that each of you have carried the "Remembrance Charm", that I gave you on the first day of class. I have one of these charms myself and it has offered me comfort through the years so I can revisit the moments I have had with my mother and father and other family members. The charm that you have is like mine. The charm has recorded video and audio of your interactions with your family. What I did not tell you was that at a later date I would give to you the playback device that will display a holographic display of your families as you interacted with them. I believe you have earned this device. It was developed by the military for its soldiers to carry into battle and could be accessed by one's superior officer to observe how well individual troops are doing and whether or not they need assistance. At the end of class today I will be giving you the playback device."

"You know you all are in a special class. You are the

smartest, brightest, and intellectually above your peers on all your performance evaluations. Consequently, because of my association with the military I have received permission to provide to you an opportunity to visit a top-secret military complex where research and development of advanced aircraft and weapons are conceived and developed. Some of you, if you choose may even have the opportunity to serve an internship with the military in assisting in the ongoing research."

The class was stunned silent. Some of the students were excited, some were apprehensive, and others were trying to comprehend how a class basically involved in the mental gymnastics of manipulating mathematical concepts of spherical mathematics turned into a field trip to an actual facility that is involved in the research and development of space travel. They were aware that in order to be in this class they all had to have a top-secret clearance, which to them was a novelty. They were advised they were never to discuss the curriculum outside of class. And, where was this facility? No one had ever heard of so much as a whisper concerning such a consortium.

Hanlee listened to her student's thoughts and understood the reluctance of some of them to not participate, especially since it involved the military. The young student's lives entirely revolved around academia and practical requirements of life in general and the military was not on their mental radar. Sadly, that will soon change.

"I know this is sudden, and it is voluntarily your decision to participate or not. Everyone willing to participate will receive a fifty percent discount on the next semester enrollment fee."

Reluctance and apprehension evaporated. All the students began talking at once. Hanlee waited a minute to regain control of the class. They must move quickly as time was of the essence.

"Okay class, lunch will be provided. I want you to leave your purses, books, backpacks, and other personal belongings in the class room. I will lock the door behind us and they will be perfectly safe. Now beginning with the back row please go outside quietly and get on the bus. As I said earlier, we will be back by four."

"Oh! One other thing I forgot to mention. You will have the opportunity to go aboard an actual training model of a space craft that is eventually going to be manufactured so you can see what the future of space travel may possibly be like in the coming years. This training model can actually fly but it is not yet ready to go into space."

All the students talked excitedly at the opportunity to see a space craft model and eagerly complied with Ricky and Hanlee's instructions. They were the last to leave. Hanlee locked the door behind them.

CHAPTER 22
WARREN JUNIOR'S CHALLENGE

Warren Jr. pulled into the driveway of his home and observed that his Dad's pickup truck was on the side of the house indicating he came home early. Evidently, his "Mom", Becky, had told him about his involvement with Alice. He really did not want to deal with him about her. It was a cut and dried deal. Alice was going to be his companion and helpmeet and wife. He knew the best way to deal with his father was to be direct.

As Alice and Warren Jr. entered the house, he observed his Father and Mother sitting at the kitchen table.

"Hi Dad, Hi Mom. I would like you to meet Alice. She is my companion and I love her very much."

Warren Jr's direct declaration to his parents surprised Warren but Becky had already met Alice at Emily's house and she stood and walked over to the young woman and gave her a hug. Alice was also aware of the subterfuge that was necessary when circumstances involved Warren.

Becky said, "Alice, it is so nice to meet you. You are welcome in our home. We have plenty of room for you. Where on earth has Warren Jr. been hiding you?"

Warren looked at the young girl who could not

possibly be over fifteen or sixteen years old at the most.

Warren said, "I do not suppose you met Warren Jr. at school unless you are in some kind of accelerated learning program. Are you?"

Alice could read his mind and she could see an underlying black field of distrust. Warren Jr. had told her what happened between his mother, Emily, and his father, and how it had become necessary to wipe his mind and memory of her and the Andrians. Becky had been chosen by Emily to be his surrogate mom and Warren's wife. Becky had always had a crush on Warren since her high school days. So, it seemed to Emily she was a good match and she agreed to be Warren's wife and Warren Jr's Mom when Emily was honest with her about what was at stake. Becky had false memory implants believing Warren was her husband and Warren Jr. was her biological son until Sara found it necessary to restore her memory. They all believed the time was short and the dreams she was having was obviously Emily trying to contact her as she had been trying to contact them.

An underlying side effect of Warren's erased memory and the implants of false memories is that he had become distrustful of strangers and did not mind letting them know it. He had become extremely adept at detecting lies and falsehoods. His way above average in intelligence required that they monitor him on a yearly basis and basically reinstall his false memories. It was getting more difficult each time they reinforced the false memories.

Alice carefully chose her words and said, "Actually no. I have not been to school in several months. I even flunked the ninth grade. We accidently ran into one another at the lake in the forest. I do not know why but we sort of hit it off. I know I am three years younger than Warren Jr. but I love him with all my heart and I cannot explain why. I have never felt anything like this before. Not only that but I have been treated for a brain tumor and was told I had only one or two more years to live. I would like for the years or time that I have left to be pleasant ones."

Everything Alice said was the absolute truth. She had been told that she had maybe two years to live. She just omitted that she had been healed by Grandma Flata.

Warren accepted the story about who she was and the circumstances of their meeting. Still she seemed so young and fragile. She looked like a flower child from the last century. Warren looked at his son. He believed him to be somewhat strange. He never dated and he certainly never brought home a girl before. Warren knew he was smart but for some reason he seemed to be an underachiever.

Warren said, "Son, do you not think you two are a little young to be talking about a lifetime commitment?" As soon as he said life time commitment he regretted his poor choice of words.

"What I mean to say is, do you love her as she loves you? And as she said, she was told she only has two years to live. Do you realize the kind of pain you both will go thru?"

"Well, I am against any kind of marriage. I am sure your mother has the same opinion as I. You are both just too young."

Becky was always careful not to go against Warren because he became angry very easily. Even though he had calming medication and worked in an oxygen rich environment in the woods he would at times seem to explode with anger.

Becky said, "Warren, I think that Warren Jr. is plenty mature to make that kind of decision. Alice can live here with us and if per chance her health turns bad, we will be her support group. It will be good for both of them. If she does not want to go to school, she does not have to. She can help me with Lilly.

And, as Becky expected, Warren had a spike of anger which he was barely able to control.

"How can you go against me on this Becky? Our son is not yet out of high school and she quit in the ninth grade. Does she even understand what love and commitment is?"

Before Becky could respond, Alice said, "I understand you loved your wife since high school and she loved you. Why should it not be any different for Warren Jr. and I. I would wager my life that if Becky was ill with a terminal disease you would not have considered it an issue."

Warren was surprised at Alice's brazen intervention between him and Becky but he was aware that her logic was sound. Of course, he would not have considered a terminal illness a hinderance to their relationship.

Warren calmed immediately. He knew he had swinging anger issues and he just could not fathom why that was the case. He was very happy. He had a good job, a beautiful wife, a wonderful son and daughter. Why was he so angry sometimes?

After dinner Warren went early to bed as was his practice and was soon fast asleep. Warren Jr. took the opportunity to explain to Becky, whom he still called Mom, and Alice, how he planned to gather together the first group of students to be evacuated. It was to be a five-day plan. Each day he would gather two hundred students from across the area encompassing several school districts under the guise of a five-day science fair outing. He already had the buses lined up and their pick-up locations assigned. None of the students was aware that he was the organizer of the event. He and Alice would just be one of the participants. In effect, he was using Hanlee's model of mass evacuation as it appeared to be the most effective. The evacuation would begin in two days. In order to get the students to participate on such short notice, they were to be given vouchers for a free first year of college tuition at the University of their choice. And these students, like Hanlee's students had been given a, "Remembrance Charm". Not only they, but all the evacuees had received the same charm.

CHAPTER 23
EXCITING EXCUSION

Sara was waiting at the front of the space craft which held up to three hundred people. The space craft was similar in concept to a bus and could easily enter the hangers of the new Intergalactic Arks. It was determined that it was not necessary to put newcomers into three-month decontamination as most all of the plants came from the earth as did all the soil. If anything, the Andrians would require inoculations for common earth diseases. And, unknown to the selected earth populations there had been an ongoing inoculations program thru the schools, universities, and employment centers that rendered earth scourges mute.

It was determined that it would take at least a year to move all the selected population to the arks. There was no way they could keep secret the disappearance of about five million people. At best estimate they could operate secretly a for about three months. When they could no longer operate in secret they would start the second phase of the project which consisted of a simulated plague where the selected individuals would appear to contract a contagious disease and they would be picked up by the military for quarantine and then the loved ones left behind would be told that selectees had died and their remains were cremated.

TARGET EARTH

The Intergalactic Ark itself was a little over one half the size of Earth's moon and elongated and disguised as such. Thus, the Ark was about eight hundred miles in diameter. The Ark was modeled after the space ship discovered by Blain and Emily years before when Blain had abducted Emily to protect her from the Andrian traitors and had taken her to the Intergalactic Carrier. Later, while they were on an excursion, Emily had found an airlock on Saturn's moon Iapetus. To their astonishment they were able to open the airlock and inside they discovered a perfectly preserved specimen of their alien enemy frozen in time. They believed it was possibly a scout who was trapped in the airlock and could not escape. There Later excursions by the military learned that the moon was in fact an artifact construct to look like a moon or asteroid.

The Iapetus space ship was dated to be at least a million years old. The Andrians studied all the star systems within artifact and did not recognize any of the myriad number of star charts. The propulsion system was ION powered and could travel near the speed of light over vast distances. They had an industrial system where they could break down the many minerals on asteroids and moons for fuel, water, and other manufacturing processes.

Using the Saturn artifact, known by humans to be the moon Iapetus, as a model for the new arks, the Andrians built their arks in the same manner. Traveling thru the cosmos it would look like any other wandering moon or space debris. It was believed that the humanoid specie that built the Iapetus Ark may well have been trying to escape the same enemy as the Andrians and the Humans are trying to escape today. The new Jupiter Ark would be a replica of the Iapetus Ark.

As the buses rounded a corner the lead bus appeared to be on a collision course with a large boulder where the road ended at the face of a mountain. But as the bus continued on the collision course it did not try to avoid colliding with the boulder which would cause a horrific accident; the boulder and surrounding forest just shimmered as the bus passed thru the camouflaged entrance disappearing from sight of the outside passengers on the other buses as it drove into the base. All the students gasped in surprise knowing full well they could easily be killed should such a collision occur.

The first bus pulled up to the space ship and Sara waited patiently until all five buses had unloaded its cargo. All the student occupants gawked at the space craft. It was long and sleek without any indication it could fly. The color was jet black and had a wide ramp that opened in the middle to provide entry.

Sara, dressed in her Space Intelligence uniform and wearing all of her commendation medals, including her sidearm, looked every inch the warrior she was. Hanlee walked over to Sara and gave her a brief hug then tuned and faced the group. With the two different uniforms, it appeared both women were in the military although different branches. But what military it was, was unknown as no one recognized the uniforms or the insignias. Also, it was sort of ominous to see ten other military types with some kind of rifle hanging from their shoulder standing at attention in the back ground.

Sara addressed the group and encouraged them to move into a tighter circle which they did. Being bunched together gave them a sense of security in the strange surroundings.

"Thank you for coming. I imagine your entry into our military base was somewhat of a dramatic surprise."

All the students laughed as it was an obvious understatement.

"Your being here is a testimony of your hard work and dedication for learning. Each of you have been vetted by your teacher, Hanlee. Because of your above average intelligence and ability to think outside the normal parameters in problem solving, each of you have been selected to participate in an experimental program. You will have opportunities and challenges to explore and expand the frontiers of knowledge. Therefore, without any further discussion I would like to invite you aboard a space craft of the future. At the end of this experimental exercise we would appreciate it if you would write us a critique on how well we did our job in providing you with a unique adventure. Please go up the ramp into the craft and take a seat. Any seat will be fine. This craft will accommodate all of you so please no pushing".

All the students did as they were told and walked up the ramp and took a seat. It was really very exciting as none of them had ever seen any space craft before. The inside of the craft looked very utilitarian. The seats were comfortable enough but not one that would be a joy sitting in for hours. There were no windows but in lieu of windows there was a large screen above the seats that allowed one an electronic view of the outside.

After the students were seated another bus arrived at the hanger and women and children got out. They too took their seats on the space craft. This process was repeated until the last fifty seats was filled. At this time the overhead screens switched from an outside view of the craft to Sara and Hanlee standing at a podium toward the front of the ship.

Sara said, "Now ladies and gentlemen, we are going to take a short excursion as a test run for the proficiency of embarkation of our space craft. Do not be alarmed. Remember, this is just a simulation. We will be home for lunch. The systems are automatic. A belt system will cross your chest. A small device will come from the overhead and a membrane will cover your nose and mouth. This will enable you to breath when we reach the simulated altitude where there is no longer any gravity or oxygen. Once we have reached the outer atmosphere and can see the curvature of the earth, we will enjoy the view for a few minutes then return to the base. And, should you be interested we will offer you options for an internship here at the facility."

The seat belts crossed the traveler's chest and a small device came down from the ceiling and covered every one's nose and mouth. Everyone took a breath and was instantly asleep.

The Andrian space transports were propelled with tachyon accelerators using quantum physics which was

TARGET EARTH

a thousand years ahead of human technology. The travel time to Jupiter using this propulsion system was three earth days. They would ride the magnetic waves into folding space. It would take only four jumps. The first Intergalactic Ark was ready and waiting in orbit beyond Jupiter's moon Ganymede, the largest moon in the solar system. The moon is three thousand two hundred and seventy-three miles across. It is larger than the planet Mercury. This location was chosen because of the huge selection and quantity of resources readily available. Ganymede has a slight magnetic field and underground oceans which also is conducive to manufacturing.

Sara exited the ship satisfied that everything went so smoothly. Hanlee took a seat next to Ricky who had previously boarded the craft and took his designated position. The family had agreed that one of them should accompany the first space ship to the ark to evaluate the efficiency of the process. Hanlee had been the chosen representative. Ricky was along because Hanlee was no stranger to the whimsical nature of space travel and thus chose not to be separated from him. Ricky was not so sure he should be glad to be along although he did love Hanlee. Before they left everyone said their goodbyes'. They too knew the vicissitudes of space travel and knew full well they may not ever see her again. Tears flowed freely. Soon they too were fast asleep.

Sara kept getting an uneasy feeling in her stomach. It was the same feeling she got when she went into combat. One time she thought someone had actually tapped her on her shoulder. She knows she definitely heard her name called from behind her back. She even turned to respond. Finally, a loud clarion echoed in her heard, "Take Hanlee off the ship!"

Sara called out startling her security force, "Get Hanlee and Ricky off the ship! Do it now before it takes off!"

Six commando members of her security force ran up the ramp into the space plane and removed Hanlee and Ricky from their seats. They were unconscious from the anesthetic gas which had been administered and would be unconscious for at least twenty-four hours. Just as the last commando stepped off the ramp, the ramp whished to a closed position in the blink of an eye and the hatchway closed like an iris.

Soon Hanlee's "would be" space craft left the hanger and more buses arrived and the selected individuals were also loaded on more space craft. And, before the sun came up the next day the number of selectees which was dispatched to the Intergalactic Ark was fifty thousand souls. The ark would leave immediately after the last candidates was on board.

Hanlee awoke from her slumber casually stretching and opening her eyes she saw Sara standing above her grinning at her. Hanlee looked around and saw Ricky asleep on the other side of the bed.

"Where am I? Am I on the ark? What are you doing here?"

Sara said, "No, you are not on the ark. I ordered my commandoes to take you and Ricky off the space craft. I believe Emily wanted you off for some reason. I actually heard a voice in my head telling me to get you off the space craft, so I did. I suspect that we will soon find out."

CHAPTER 24
HIGH SCHOOL OUTING DELIGHT SEVEN DAYS BEFORE INVASION

Warren Jr. and Alice stood in the mist of the first group of two-hundred students in the parking lot of the Pantry Mart, the largest retail outlet within a hundred miles. All of the students were excited because they were told that the first part of the science fair included a visit to a military base that was predominantly space oriented. A hand out was circulated that said the students would get to visit a control center for launching military rockets that was responsible for putting satellites into orbit and providing supplies to the five new space stations. It also said something about them going aboard a mockup of a new space shuttle that ferried astronauts to and from the space stations. After visiting the mock-up of the space shuttle, they were going to have lunch in the cafeteria with real live astronauts! This was absolutely more than any of them expected!

The five buses arrived right on time. None of the students did not think twice to ask where the adult teachers were. They just believed they would be along and were travelling by their own private vehicles. Warren Jr. had arranged for the teachers to be at their own seminar in New York with all expenses payed for by the military. Before they were to return to their classes their mind would be wiped and they would have no memory of the missing students and they would be assigned to other classes. Warren Jr. was pleased with himself at arranging such a large- scale abduction. And, an abduction is exactly what it was even if it was for saving the human race. Fortunately, all the students were living on campus and the parents would not miss them for some time, perhaps not until the next semester.

Alice sat next Warren Jr. on a bench enthralled at being part of such an important endeavor. Snuggling up to Warren Jr., Alice said, "I would never have believed such happiness was possible for me last month when I was told that I only had a year to live. I am afraid that something awful is going to take it away. I have been living under a cloud of despair for so long and I had to make myself enjoy the so many small things that make life beautiful, most of which we take for granted."

"When trying to live my life to the fullest I found refuge in my music. Music was the only thing that would lift my spirits and allow me to thank the Great God of The Universe, for giving the so many pleasures I enjoyed. And, the greatest gift of all is you."

Alice kissed Warren Jr's shoulder and walked forward with the crowd of students and listened to them excitedly expound to one another what a marvelous opportunity this science fair was going to be. And to think they were going to get the opportunity go to a secret military base and go aboard an actual rocket trainer to meet real live astronauts and ask questions!

Once the buses came to a stop next to the mockup of a real rocket transport, everyone excitedly got out of the buses and formed a semi-circle around a young woman in a military uniform. She looked so exotic. She had a side arm strapped to her leg and if one looked close enough you could spot two small knives adhering to her lower legs on her calf.

One of the young men looked at Sara and he immediately and inexorably fell in love with her. She was beautiful. She was strong. She was so exotic! She was everything any man could ever want in a woman He did not care if he was only fifteen and she was a much older woman!

Sara was caught unawares and the "much older woman" moniker caught her completely by surprise. Well, sometimes it would be wiser not to read minds. She looked at the young man having read his mind. He already had a bad case of hero worship. Looking him in the eye she entered his mind and said, "What a fine young man you are. Wish I was fifteen again."

The young man turned beat red mesmerized that she spoke to him not understanding that the communication had been telepathic. Sara smiled at him and then addressed the group.

"Thank you all for coming. This is going to be an exciting science fair. After we visit this replica of a space transport, we will go have lunch in the cafeteria. After lunch we will divide you up into different teams. You may not choose whom you wish to team up with because we are well aware of your skills and we will match accordingly. You should know that the winning team will be awarded a ride to a space station where you will be an integral part of the space station crew and work alongside astronauts conducting live experiments and may even be given the chance for a spacewalk, should you desire."

Everyone laughed and cheered talking excitedly as they followed Sara up the ramp. Warren Jr. and Alice lagged behind and no one noticed when they casually walked away from the group.

Alice looked up at Warren Jr. with solemn blue eyes and tears beginning to collect at the corner of her eyes.

"What is going to happen to them Warren? Will they be okay?"

Warren responded with a hard edge in his voice, "They are going to have a chance to live. That is more than the rest of the people on the earth will have ".

CHAPTER 25
ENLIGHTEN THE LEADERSHIP

Sara, her father, Commander Sears, and Andrian Commander Taaker was leading a group of military leaders and scientist on a discussion on how to alert the general population of the imminent threat of an Alien invasion by beings from a different dimension. There was pro and cons to enlighten or keep ignorant until the day of the arrival, or the beginning of the end of life on earth.

It was a majority vote that humankind should be told of the calamity which was soon to be upon them. Everyone believed that the cataclysmic event would not happen for at least another generation. However, due to the strong dream impressions they were all having, they believed that the decision to load and launch seed ships immediately was the most correct defensive action against total annihilation. Thus, the programs had begun. The first seed ship was launched from Jupiter with a complete complement of fifty thousand Humans and Andrians on a multi-generational trip to parts of the universe unknown. The young people on the ship were in suspended animation and would not awaken for at least one hundred years. All the ships controls were robotically controlled. When they awaken, they will be the same age as when they boarded the craft.

Commander Sears said, "We should begin by contacting the numerous survivalist groups in the Associate States. And, we must be honest with them and advise them what we all are up against. And, most importantly we should provide them with all the weapons and ammunition they can use. If we are to be destroyed from the face of the earth, we should not make it easy for the invaders."

Commander Taaker advised, "There is an investigative journalist that has written extensively about these groups and has visited many of their training camps. Since she does not trash them in her articles, she has gained a respectful following and they feed her tips and leads pertaining to government corruption and cover-ups. In fact, she was investigating us at one point in time and that is how we are aware of her work. We were able to assure her that nothing of consequence was going on here. Of course, that was with a bit of intrusion."

Everyone laughed at Commander Taaker's humor. He did not have much humor and one could see his assimilation into human culture did not come easily to him.

Sara thought for a minute and then asked if it would be possible for him to set up a meeting with the journalist.

"What is her name, do you recall?", asked Sara.

Sara realizing her error said in a smiling manner, "Sorry Commander, of course you remember. You have a photographic memory, at least compared to us Humans."

Again, everyone laughed as Sara acknowledged Andrian superiority of mental intellect over Humans.

"Yes, her name is Charlene James. She is your age. Maybe you know her? Oh, I forgot, you did not go to high school, did you? You had that unfortunate turn of events when you went aboard an Intergalactic Carrier at age twelve."

Sara snorted, "Why Commander Taaker, I believe you have become more Human than you thought possible."

Everyone in the group laughed.

Commander Taaker grinned at her and said, "It appears so, Commander. Do you want me to bring her here or meet her elsewhere?"

I want to meet her at her, at our would be high school. You know the one. It is the one which I did not get to attend and missed my senior prom".

"My, my, commander. Do I detect a hint of deep-seated anger? You know we do have counselors for that kind of affliction. If you like we can implant memories of what a wonderful time you had." Commander Taaker grinned at her.

"You know what Commander, you are so full of yourself! I think I prefer you a little less assimilated."

Truth be known, Sara had come to love Commander Taaker almost as much as she loved her father. And, Commander Taaker, having no children of his own had come to love Sara as if she was his daughter.

Again, everyone laughed and enjoyed the byplay.

"Ok Commander, set up the meeting as soon as possible. I just feel we must go with all haste."

"Yes Commander, it will be attended to immediately."

Commander Taaker and Sara's Father, Commander Sears, left together. They had become an inseparable team.

CHAPTER 26
STRANGE VISITORS

Charlene James had just received a phone call about strange things going on in the North Eastern part of the Associate States. There were reports of strange lights in the skies and lights underwater of the Great Lakes. And, for heaven sakes, there were also reports of mermaids seen off the coast. The call was anonymous.

Mumbling to herself she said, "They must think I am a fool".

At that thought the doorbell rang. Strange, it was five in the evening. No one ever comes by at this time of the early evening. Charlene James thought that perhaps she just would not answer the door, after all, she had not had her first glass of wine.

The doorbell rang again and this time it was more persistent.

Again thinking, "I have been sort of short on cash lately. What if it is a job offer?"

At that thought she jumped up and went to the door. Upon opening the door, she observed two very large men in military uniforms. She recognized the ruggedly handsome one immediately. Then she recognized the other man, she had labeled him the strange one.

"Ms. Charlene James, may we come in? We have a proposal for you which could be very lucrative for you, even up to a years' salary, if not more."

Charlene opened the door wider. She was just curious as to why these two particular men had sought her out. The offer of money could be a double-edged sword. One should be aware of Greeks bearing gifts.

Both men came into the house and walked to the living room. The walls were covered with different stories which she had worked on. In the corner they observed a story about flying saucers, in their neighborhood no less.

Charlene James thought again, "Beware of Greeks bearing gifts".

"Okay, why are you here? The last time I saw you two you were talking about going fishing and invited me along. What is this about money, in any size and denomination; a whole years' salary no less?"

"Thank you for being direct and wanting to get to the point. No doubt that attitude has served you well in your investigative journalist career", said the strange one.

"We understand you have a rapport with many of the survivalist groups. Our Commander has sent us out to find you and bring you back with us to meet and greet you. We will deposit one years' salary into your account if you will just come and listen.", said the handsome one.

Charlene James was instantly angry as she believed they wanted her to betray the confidences for which she labored so diligently over the years.

Angrily she said, "You can get out! I will never betray those who have trusted me over the years. You cannot pay me enough to do so! It hurts my soul to think you believe that I would do so!"

Commander Sears said, "Believe me when I say, I understand integrity. We both do.", Indicating Commander Taaker.

"It is because of your integrity that we contacted you instead of other journalist", Commander Sears said hopefully mollifying her anger into a more receptive mood.

"You misunderstood our statement that we would pay you to accompany us to betray the trust of those Citizens who are most dear to us. The money is just to pay you for your inconvenience in coming with us right now. We have a plane waiting. The meeting will be in your old high school. That is the location our Commander chose. You will not need anything but your purse, computer, and cell phone."

Charlene James looks suspiciously at the two men.

"Fine, I will go with you but I am going to call my mom and let her know where I am going and with whom."

"That is fine", Said Commander Taaker

Commander Taaker then took her arms and looked into her eyes and said, "You are asleep but you can walk on your own, and you did talk to your mom."

Charlene James opened her eyes in surprise but she saw nothing.

CHAPTER 27
MUTUAL FRIENDS

Sara was waiting in the cafeteria of the closed school. There was the usual security team standing in the corners and outside the building. It was six P.M. when Commanders Sears and Taaker entered the room with Charlene James. She walked in a straight line like she was told to do and came to a stop in front of Sara.

Sara said, "You can wake up now. You were so tired that you slept the whole flight".

Charlene woke up dazed and confused. Looking around she was surprised to find herself in her high school cafeteria.

"How did I get here? I do not remember anything."

Sara indicated for Charlene to sit down at a table that was carefully set with tomato soup, French bread and a bottle of red wine.

Sara looked her in the eye and said, "We manipulated your memory and put you to sleep. Time is of the essence and we want to have you fresh and alert once we began to solicit your cooperation in contacting as many survivalist groups as possible. After what we have to tell you and you perchance choose not to participate then you will be free to go. We promise not to wipe your mind of what you learned, and, we will deposit an additional years' salary into your account, and of course expect your silence as to the content of our meeting."

Charlene James looked closely at the young woman. She was thinking, "Can they really wipe my memories? Evidently, they can because the last thing I remembered was talking to my Mom, or did I?"

They appeared to be about the same age. She was wearing a military uniform with several combat ribbons on her chest. And yes, strangely enough, there was a sea star on thinly woven green strands of some kind of material that looked like sea weed, hanging around her neck. It appeared to go with a gold starfish braided into her hair. How odd.

Her face had fine lines like knife wounds on her cheek and the tip of her ear was missing. Her hands were gracefully laying on one another on the table and they looked like they had been broken in a thousand pieces.

Looking from Sara to her surroundings she saw several men and women in military uniforms similar to the young woman's. She did not know what branch of the service they belonged too. They were all carrying some kind of weapon of which she was not familiar. That was strange because she had an encyclopedic knowledge of all firearms and weapons. They stood discreetly within the dark recess of the hanging curtains.

In addition to the soldiers she could see the silhouette of a very tall women in strange clothing. Her features were vague in the diminished light but her long, flowing, red hair hanging past her shoulders was clearly visible. She too was wearing a sidearm.

Sara picked up the bottle of red wine and pored them

each a glass. It wasn't lost on Charlene James that the wine was her favorite as was the soup and bread. She doubted there was not much they did not know about her.

Sara said, I know two young ladies you went to school with. They were my friends in elementary school and the seventh and eighth grade; their names are Haley and Kyla.

Charlene James looked shocked. "You knew Haley? I mean she was my best friend in high school. By all the sacred stars, I miss her so much!"

It was Sara's turn to be taken aback. "By all the sacred stars", was their secret pact words of friends forever. A small tear came unbidden to her eye. She too missed Haley and she had not thought of her for years.

Charlene James notices the unbidden tear and knew that despite the woman's hardened exterior she had a soft heart, at least she hoped she did.

"My name is Sara Sears. I think you have already met my dad, Commander Sears. He is standing over in the corner with Commander Taaker. Yeah, I know Commander Taaker is somewhat strange by earth standards but he would give the flesh off his bones to see that you are safe."

Charlene James felt uncomfortable with the metaphor. How gruesome.

"I love him as my surrogate dad and he thinks of me as his daughter as he has no children of his own. Actually, he is developing a sense of humor, he is being assimilated quite nicely."

Sara quickly changed the subject and said, "I think we also have a mutual friend in Kyla. Have you seen her lately? She has two beautiful children. She married a lawyer and now they have a very lucrative practice downtown organizing and dispensing military contracts."

Charlene James sat furiously thinking taking a minute trying to put the pieces together. Finally, she had it. "You are that Sara that disappeared for years. They were always talking about you. I guess Haley never had a chance to see you come back from where ever you went. She was murdered by that evil man she was going with. He even got away with killing her saying it was an accident. His family was very powerful."

Sara smiled and in a voice that became hard said, "Actually they did not get away with it. They all died in a fire."

"Yes, but dying in an accidental fire is not justice to me. It just does not seem right."

Sara responded with, "You know, Haley was not the only young girl he murdered. There were eight more. However, their parents did receive closure as did Haley's parents."

Charlene James sat quietly trying to judge wither this woman named Sara was telling the truth or not. She certainly seemed credible; and how strange that they should meet after all these years and have mutual friends?

"I will tell you how they died. They were all gathered around a table discussing how they were going to defraud millions from a hospital and a charity, out of their money. I secretly entered their compound and threw an advanced neural neutralizer into the room. They were frozen in place not able to move so much as an eye muscle. I then pitched a type of weapon that emitted a gas and when inhaled caused the subjects to burn from the inside out, starting very slowly. You know, to prolong the agony. They burned like candles sitting in their seats unable to move. I then sent a video of their deaths to each of the parents that had children that were murdered by Haley's boyfriend."

Charlene James sat with her mouth open. Sara had just confessed to murdering a whole family. Why had she told her that she had done this thing and what kind of woman was she that she had access to these exotic weapons? She was becoming confused. There were so many questions.

Suddenly Charlene James blurted out saying, "Why did you bring me here? Who are you people?"

Sara smiled. "I was beginning to think you were never going to ask."

Sara leaned forward with the glass of wine in her hand and said, "The earth and every man, woman and child on the planet is going to be destroyed by alien entities from a different dimension. We do not know how much time we have but we think it is at least one generation. We do not know for sure because we have all been receiving these dreams and premonitions of something is going to happen. We believe that these dreams are efforts by Commander Emily Smith to warn us of an impending disaster. Because of these premonitions, if you will, we have launched the first intergalactic ship with fifty thousand young people to parts unknown in the galaxy. We have done this because we are trying to save a remnant of the Human and Andrian species. All life on earth will be destroyed if we cannot stop them. As of this moment we have been unable to do so, not because we cannot kill them but they are innumerable and their casualties are not an issue to them. If we are to be destroyed, we want to inflict as much pain and suffering on these alien things as possible. We will all fight to the death. Now you know why we need you to contact the survivalist and have them help us organize a resistance. They will not believe us but they will believe you. So, are you in, or, are you out?"

"I would like you to meet someone who's world was destroyed along with all but twenty-six of her specie. They were fighting to the death on a small atoll when Commander Emily Smith and several Space Intelligence Commandoes landed a saucer and saved them.

The tall redheaded woman walked from the shadows and stood before Charlene James. She was very Muskular. Charlene was surprised when she heard a voice in her head.

"Hello, my name is Muskula. I am or was the leader of the Great Sea Star people. We are an aquatic specie. I believe you call us mermaids. It is a mystery how some of our people appeared on old earth ages ago. On our world, we numbered as the grains of sand in the sea. That is until the alien nemesis arrived and destroyed us from our home. We fought them for many moon cycles. It did not matter how many we killed. They poured from the sky like a deluge of never-ending rain. If it was not for Emily Smith and the Andrians, we would have been totally wiped from existence. Thus, we humbly seek your assistance in establishing an organized resistance."

Muskula then returned to her initial position next to the wall.

Charlene James sat frozen in her seat with the wine half way to her mouth. She was a professional investigative reporter. She could smell a lie or detect subterfuge from any source. She was born with an innate sense of truth. She did not want to believe this woman Sara or, oh for heaven's sakes, that woman that was a mermaid! Her heart screamed that it was a lie. That, it was not real! The words they spoke was an elaborate plan to discredit her in some unknown way. But every cell in her body screamed that it was the truth. She could not breath.

It took several moments for Charlene James to collect her senses. She was in a form of shock. She looked away swallowing hard several times. Tears trickled down her cheeks. Thinking to herself she thought, "Congratulations. You just got the biggest investigative report in history! The total annihilation of the Human Race!"

Sara, reading Charlene James' mind was well aware of her anguish of soul. She understood the process well. She would never be able to count the tears she herself had shed. She had been a good friend to Haley and to Kyla. There will be room for her on a seed ship should she wish to go.

Sara said, "Be at peace Charlene James. We will make this work."

CHAPTER 28
MEETING OF ANGELS

Emily did not know how many gravity waves she traversed or how many times she manipulated folding space. She only knew there had to be some kind of higher form of being other than herself and the space craft entity, and she needed desperately to find them. There was no doubt in her mind the earth and all the inhabitants were going to be destroyed by the alien entity from a different dimension. Not only that, all life forms in their dimension and universe is being destroyed. Surly the Supreme Being of the Universe will not allow that to happen. But why has nothing been done?

Emily moved steadily in one direction. She could not explain why she chose the direction in which she moved. It just seemed right. It also seemed to be getting brighter although that could be her imagination.

Since she was no longer a corporeal being, she did not feel thirst or hunger. She did not sense cold or heat. She did have the awesome power to have vision which encompassed every direction at once. Of course, the vision was not like that of a corporeal being as she could see and taste quarks, atoms, and each and every particle ever created. She could view her surroundings in every frequency of light. Not only that, she could hear the songs of the universe. Every star, planet, moon and all creation had its' own vibration. Together the vibrations made music that was unlike anything she had ever heard. It was beautiful.

"Emily! Emily! Come this way!"

Emily was unsure she heard her name but the musical tones seemed to her to call her name. She seemed instinctively to know which way to go. And in that that particular direction, the aurora of light seemed to be getting brighter.

Emily could see a large shimmering wall that appeared to stretch to both sides as far as her vision allowed her to see. The height and depth of the wall matched its' horizontal likeness. Emily saw what appeared to be points of light moving in her direction. As they came closer, they morphed into winged creatures of pure light with sapphires and emeralds glowing in the mist of the heavenly creatures. There were so many of them and they encompassed themselves around about her and together they moved toward the shimmering, opaque wall.

As they neared the wall a portal opened and they entered the portal to the other side. Emily was astounded by the beauty within the enclosed boundary of the wall. Looking back toward the wall she observed what appeared to be a multitude of huge magnifiers which allowed one to peer toward different planets, throughout the universe. Indeed, she saw what appeared to be the planet earth but how could that be possible. Then she remembered that, "With God all things are possible."

The angelic beings escorted Emily to a large edifice with different frequencies of light emanating from the building. They stopped before a large door that opened and the beings indicated that Emily should continue, alone.

Emily entered the room through a tunnel of bright white light and came to the base of a multi stepped alter with a large golden colored chair on the top. The chair was unoccupied.

Off to the side Emily heard a voice say, "Emily, come here."

Emily moved toward the voice rounding the corner of the alter. She saw a Being of the most beautiful light displaying a kaleidoscope of all the frequencies of light. Emily fell to her knees at the sheer majesty of the Being. She tried to filter her various visual sensors for the light but was unable to do so. With omni vision that allowed senses to see in all directions turning her back to limit the light did not help.

"Your light is too pure; I cannot look at you!"

Immediately Emily received a reduction of force which the light emitted and she was at ease. Indeed, Emily had never experienced such peace.

"We have been waiting for you. We have heard all your prayers. The Evil One has opened the bottomless pit and released the lifeforms that has wreaked havoc in Our Universe. We are aware of your valor and have seen your efforts to save other species."

"Because your knowledge and understanding is limited and your vision is near non-existent, you are unable to make a definitive assessment of the spiritual realm. This is by design. It was not your time to receive this understanding. Now that calamity is upon the universe you will be tested unto death. You will all pass from the earth blind and transverse to the light of understanding at the very moment that a physical death is at your door."

"Some will be allowed to remain and battle the evil entity until the very moment that death is upon them. But in that moment, we shall remove them from their enemy's grasp."

"We will do this because the enemy, unlike you, have all spiritual knowledge and understanding. They will immediately know that their reign of terror and death has come to an end and their fate is sealed. They will have nothing but fear and trembling until that moment in time when the last millisecond is ended. They will see the universe roll up as a scroll and rush toward them. And in the instant the scroll of light and truth meets them their existence will be as if it never was. The dark matter that is left surrounding them will propel them to a bottomless pit of never-ending darkness. They will be individually separated, each in its own realm. They will see and hear nothing from the outside but they will always see each of the individual souls they destroyed, and then see them receive an abundance of rewards which would have been theirs if only they had not listened to the Evil One."

Emily experienced so many emotions upon hearing these things she could only remain on her knees and prostrate herself toward the Spiritual Being.

The Being then said, "I have created a new heaven and a new earth and each and every soul removed from the old will be placed in the new."

"But tell me Emily Smith, I see another within your spirit which I did not create. From whence did this being come?"

The machine entity which was part of Emily was about to speak but Emily commanded, "Entity! Be silent before our God!"

Emily knew what the Entity was going to say and she was fairly sure that the words would not be well received by the superior Spiritual Being.

Emily responded by saying, "It may be true you yourself did not create this part of my Spirit, however, the Andrian scientist that did create the biological mechanical being, is also your creation, thus by default, this creation is yours also. However, forgive me for being presumptuous for presenting such a posit before you, my Lord!"

The Spiritual Being said, "I want this Andrian individual brought before me so I may inquire of her why she has done this thing."

Emily was fearful in heart for Flata. "Had it not been for Flata's creation, I would never have had the opportunity to save two different species from the evil ones nor would I be here before you today, my Lord!"

"That is true. And, that is why I wish to meet this Human that can do such things."

"She is not Human my Lord. She is not from the planet earth. She is Andrian. She is humanoid having the same physic as we but due to circumstances beyond her control, she was required to make many decisions that affected her species. They, as a species, are much more intelligent than humans. She, as most of her specie, has lived their life aboard an Intergalactic Spacecraft traveling the cosmos. She has never set foot on a planet until recently when she came to earth."

"Bring her to me. I will give you the power to do so."

"Yes, my Lord. I will do as you command."

CHAPTER 29
A TIME TO WEEP, A TIME TO MOURN

Orion and Perilain was sitting on Emily's porch and they were discussing how to freeze a time warp and see if it was possible to go thru the tunnel without being looped back to the beginning of the experiment. The discussion was purely academic with no basis in fact. Even though both boys now had the equivalent of a doctorate in theoretical physics, they did not look down upon their cousins that did not have the same mental abilities as they. All of the cousins were way above the norm of the general human population and every one of them were exceptional students when it came to spherical mathematics.

Warren Jr. and Alice listened in on the conversation fascinated at the suppositions the two fifteen-year old boys were proposing. They bounced ideas off of one another and dissected theorems like a skilled surgeon using a laser knife to dissect a frog.

Flata sat silently in the background observing all the children. There were now six in all with Eve being the youngest at thirteen. Sara and Jawane came and sat on the porch beside her. Hanlee, Ricky, and Tiffaney sat in the yard next to the porch in the shade of a large spruce tree. Everything was idyllic and could have come from a Norman Rockwell painting some two hundred years earlier in time.

Flata sighed with happiness not having known such contentment in all the years on the Intergalactic Carrier. Life on a planet is so much easier. All of the children had benefitted one way or another by Grandma Flata's skilled acumen. The word "Grandma" had to her become the most beautiful word she could think of.

Alice resting her head on Warren Jr's shoulder asked, "Warren, where do you think the Seed Carrier is now?"

Warren Jr. replied, "The Carrier is at least five light years from the earth but we do not know in which direction it went after leaving the solar system. That was part of the plan when the system was devised. It was made that way just in case the enemy could access our communications. For better or for worse they are on their own."

Due to the urgency of Sara's premonition the Carrier was launched within twenty-four hours after loading.

Sara was looking out toward the sloping field which ended at the water's edge of the great lake inlet. She too felt in a melancholy mood enjoying the very few moments of peace with all her family. They seldom gathered in the same place at the same time. Even now they were not all there.

The air shimmered and there was a loud whooshing sound and suddenly a visual image of Emily floating in the air above the ground appeared and seemed to coalesce in and out of view. Everyone sat frozen in-place not able to speak or to move. There also appeared to be several beings of light round about her.

The image spoke. "Be at peace family. Everything will be okay. We are all going to be fine. It just will not be according to our wills but the will of the Eternal Cosmic Spirit. We are to continue fighting. The enemy will be destroyed but not by us. The reason we cannot destroy the enemy we are fighting is because it is a creation of God's enemy, the Angle of Light. In the Cosmic Spirits time our enemy will be thrown into the abyss with the enemy's creator. There will come a fine "Point of no Time", that we will all be together. Be not afraid. You know that I love you. You are to love one another."

"Now, I have been allowed to return here to deliver Grandma Flata, to the Creator of all things. The great Cosmic Spirit desires to commune with her."

As Emily said this, Flata gracefully floated from her chair toward the image of Emily.

"I do not know at this moment if she will return to you. I do know you will see her again at the "Point of no Time". Please believe me when I tell you she will be fine. You all will be fine."

Flata passed through the shimmer into Emily's arms and the vision or apparition faded. Then, everything was as it was before the appearance except Grandma Flata was no longer present. Birds could be heard singing in the distance.

No one spoke as all were in shock. They all heard Emily's voice delivering a message about Grandma Flata, but each and every one of them received a personal message a s a catch of data was transmitted into their minds.

All the military and certain of her friends each received some kind of communication. The communication was not limited to earth but Blain and Sasha also received their own personal messages, as did the men and women on the Intergalactic Carriers fighting the enemy. There was also a special message for the young people on the Seed Ship hurtling thru space. When they awoke, they would know the message by heart and understand why they were chosen to be representatives of earths' finest.

The silence was broken when Perilain said, "Orion, what is the "Point of no Time"?

CHAPTER 30
MESSAGES RECEIVED

Blain and Sasha was fighting a desperate battle in the corridor of the Intergalactic Carrier. The enemy had somehow guessed their coordinates and projected movements and managed to open a space time warp onto the ship. Fortunately for them the Captain of the Carrier had already entered different coordinates and moved to the new location. The time warp then dumped the majority of the enemy entity into deep space. Those that did make it on board inflicted many casualties among the crew personnel but the on-board security was in the process of quickly eliminating them.

Sasha was in her acid resistant armor and was easily defeating her enemy by firing her new wave laser generator weapon that sent lasers out in a horizontal beam clearing the passageway by slicing the enemy entity in half. The frequency of the laser was tuned to the molecular density of the enemy bodies thus the beam did not affect Humans or Andrians.

Flying robotic vacuum containers sucked up the acid and cleared the vapor from the battle areas. The acid fumes were then dumped into space as was the enemy bodies which was also collected by semi-sentient robotic constructs of various kinds. Of course, Sasha was successful only because the influx of the enemy was thwarted by cutting the space time warp into the carrier. Had the Captain not been able to cut the space time warp and successfully move to new coordinates, eventually the enemy would have overcome the resistance due to sheer numbers and everyone on board would be dead.

Blain and Sasha met after it was determined that no further invasion of the carrier was imminent. It was the closest any Intergalactic Carrier in their battle group had come to being destroyed. However, other individual Intergalactic Carriers have been destroyed.

Both had showered and dressed in the new daily uniforms that was somewhat acid resistant but not near as effective as the battle uniforms they had been wearing earlier. They were in the process of being refurbished for future engagements.

"Blain, I love you with my life. I thought there for a while that it might be shorter than I planned. The incursion happened so fast. I do not understand how our random coordinates were compromised."

"Sasha, you are right. The Entity within the Carrier should not have let that happen. I do not think I am going to sleep as easy as I have been in the past. I do not understand how come the other three Carriers that was compromised and destroyed along with their crew of five thousand personnel in each ship, could not break the time warp. Maybe we are asking the wrong question. The question should be is, how did we break the time warp and escape? That information is vital to our battle group."

"We know that once the enemy gains access to its

target it has never failed to succeed in achieving its objective. Perhaps the molecular Emily had a hand in breaking the time warp. We need to go to the control room and meet with the Captain."

Before leaving their quarters, they hugged each other gently for a long time followed by a soft kiss. They both realized how close they came to being destroyed. The only way to stay alive with this enemy was to stay as far away as possible while fighting them all the way to planet earth.

As they were preparing to leave the confines of their quarters, they were stunned to see a vision of Emily standing before them. She was so close they could have reached out and touched her. Her personage seemed to fade in and out and had an effervescent quality. She was smiling her beautiful lopsided smile.

"Hello beloved. I do not know how it is possible for me to be here but I just met with the most beautiful Spiritual Being ever! I cannot even begin to explain how that was possible either. Nor do I understand how it is possible for me to be here now. I do know, she said, "She would give me the power to go pick up Flata and bring her to the abode where the Spiritual Being resides." Part of me is in the process of doing that now."

"I have seen the children and visited with them. They are growing up so fast. Orion and Perilain are, as usual, discussing quantum physics and time warps."

"My son, Warren Jr., has met his soul mate. Her name is Alice. Grandma Flata cured her of a fatal inoperative brain tumor. She plays the guitar and sings folk songs popular about two centuries ago. Warren Jr. also was instrumental in assisting in launching the first seed ship with fifty thousand souls, as was all the children."

"Sara and Jawane are inseparable when duties do not require them to be elsewhere. Sara is still close to her friend Kyla and they are watched over diligently. Kyla and her husband have two children."

"Hanlee was camping and brutally assaulted by two men and they hit her on the back of her head as she was trying to escape. She fell unconscious into the river where she was rescued by a young man named Ricky and his daughter Tiffany. He became her savior and soul mate."

"Warren and Becky have a little girl named Lilly, so Warren Jr. is enjoying the role of big brother."

The Great Cosmic Spirit advised that we ourselves will not be able to destroy our Enemy. However, the Enemy will be destroyed and placed in a great void along with the Great Cosmic Spirits', Immortal Enemy, The Angel of Light."

"We should continue to battle them all the way to the earth. In effect, we have been selected and are being used to draw the Enemy to its final destruction. When their fleets arrive at earth, the beginning of "The Point of No Time" will be upon them and there will be no escape. That is when the enemy will realize that they were lured into a cosmic trap and they know they are going to be destroyed from this universe. At that moment of "The Point of No Time", we will be removed from this universe and placed in a realm prepared for us called a New Heaven and a New Earth. The individuals that have escaped earth prior to the enemy's arrival in the Intergalactic Carriers, will be translated to this new dimension. It was the same thing that happened to Moses and Elijah, they did not die, they were translated and they were removed from the earth to perform other services for The Supreme Being. Thus, those translated will be the progenitors of the new Human Species. We ourselves will become their guardians. We may be their spiritual guardians or their physical guardians.

"How this transition comes about is up to you. The time and circumstance will present itself leaving you to determine your fate. I leave you with this knowledge to give you peace." Then Emily shimmered out of existence and they were left alone in their quarters.

Blain and Sasha held each other close. They were both shivering not knowing exactly why. The message from Emily was both exhilarating and cryptic. Why was she cryptic on how they became guardians to the translated survivors of the Intergalactic Carriers and Seed Ships? However the guardianship comes about it involves two choices or plans; Plan A or Plan B. What did these plans entail?

Sasha looked up at Blain with tears in her eyes and said, "Emily said "we", which includes her. She has become a spiritual being. If we are to be like her, a spiritual being, then that means we must die. We will have a choice on how that death will come about.

Blain looked down at Sasha with love in his heart bleeding up into the softness of his eyes.

"Sasha, we are warriors. We cannot count the number

of engagements we have been in together and survived never even giving death a second thought. That is just what we do. And, when that moment comes, we will be sure we are together and together we shall enter eternity. What an exciting opportunity to be guardians in the new world to come!"

"Our primary military goal from this time forth is to stall the enemy as long as possible so Sara and the others can evacuate as many people as can be crammed into the Intergalactic Carriers. I am sure there is an equal mix of Human and Andrian. A new species will be born from this union!"

CHAPTER 31
PREPARING DEFENSE

Charlene James walked out of the woods into the clearing and followed the rugged dirt road toward a cluster of small wooden, weather worn, buildings. She knew these buildings was a decoy erected to dissuade interest in the area. Past the buildings was a moderately sized hill with a large stand of trees that camouflaged the hidden entrance to the mine. The mine access led to the base of the survivalist camp. The camp was currently occupied by representatives of the leadership of the resistance movement of the North and South Americas.

As Charlene James approached the entrance a woman came out from the trees and she was carrying an automatic assault rifle. She pointed the rifle toward the ground in front of Charlene James.

The woman stated in a loud voice, "Who are you and what do you want? I have never seen you around here before".

"Nor I you.", replied Charlene James.

"I am here to meet with the organizers and commanders of the resistance movement. They are expecting me. My name is Charlene James."

"We have been expecting you. How did you get here, we did not see any vehicle such as a truck or car approach nor was there any planes in the area? You just walked out of the woods and now here you are."

Charlene James smiled and said, "Yes. Well I sorta arrived by unconventional means which I will explain later. Right now, I need to speak to Frank Morningstar and everyone else he has assembled."

Without speaking the woman turned and walked back into the trees. Charlene James followed and came to an entrance of an old mine. Once in the mine the temperature dropped an easy ten degrees causing her to have a chill. After her eyes became accustomed to the darkness as there was not any lighting past the entrance into the mine, Charlene James saw the woman sitting in a golf cart type conveyance. Getting into the cart was not difficult as it did not have a top. The woman started driving immediately after turning on her headlights which were very dim.

After a ten-minute drive which seemed to go downhill into the mine, they exited into the sunlight which was diminished by a large number of tall trees growing on almost vertical rocky slopes. The area was large as a football field divided by a small leisurely flowing spring fed stream. The area was very idyllic and presented a nice green pasture with knee high grass for cattle to graze upon.

The very overhead center of the otherworldly vista showed a small patch of blue sky partly covered with smooth white clouds as they flowed from one side of the mountain to the other. The sky clashed with the late fall colors of the heavily forested ravine. Charlene James stood mesmerized with the view. Closing her eyes, she could smell the dampness of the stream which never ceased flowing and the water laden air clung to her clothes.

A familiar deep gravelly voice ended her reverie as Frank Morningstar called her name.

"Charlene James, I sure hope that your urgent message is important enough for me to call this unprecedented meeting. If I did not know you, I would believe this meeting is a government conspiracy to arrest us all in one big elaborate sting operation."

Charlene James looked at Frank Morningstar. Frank was a native American and he had the cole black hair and dark eyes of his native ancestry. He was heavily muscled and looked every inch the Hollywood version of his people portrayed on screen. He was ten years older than she and as far as she knew, he was not married. But who is to know?

She knew he had served in the military special forces and had engaged in military combat on many occasions. He had several knife wounds on his biceps and a crooked nose broken in several places. To round out his rugged looks his light, rose colored lips was partly open and showed two rows of straight, white teeth, with the exception of a front chipped tooth. Strange what one would notice when under great stress

He was taken aback when he saw a somber Charlene James just staring at him. He then noticed the tears flowing from her eyes dripping from her chin. She did not show any other emotion or movement. She looked sad. He had never seen her without a smile or without a glint of challenge in her eyes. She looked defeated and it did not become her.

Frank stepped forward with his arms open and scooped Charlene James into his arms and snuggled her close. As soon as his arms closed around her, she heaved great big sobs and wailed in loud despair. She could no longer hold back the shock of learning that everyone on the earth was going to die. He held her on her feet for several minutes before she regained her composure.

Several men and women had gathered round and those that knew her were equally perplexed at her great emotional breakdown. There was really no other way to describe it.

After several minutes Charlene James collected her wits about her and was totally embarrassed for her outburst.

"I am so sorry Frank. I am an emotional wreck. I know you have some whiskey around here somewhere, maybe I could have a drink?"

Everyone turned and walked to a clearing and a young woman approached her and gave her a fifth of whiskey, saying, "Keep it."

They all sat on chairs and stumps common in outdoor settings and waited until Charlene James had taken two long swallows. The young woman that had given her the bottle sat down beside her and placed her arm round about her shoulders. They appeared to be the same age.

Everyone silently looked at her expectantly. Those that knew her were somewhat apprehensive not knowing for sure if they wanted to hear what she had to say.

All the others were eager to hear what she had to say and figured it was really of no import.

Frank Morningstar waited until she seemed to be breathing comfortably and for the whiskey to calm her down. Charlene looked out over the group and searched the crowd of about hundred men and women that were close and several hundred more that flowed out onto the grasslands. All of them looked hard and their faces did not appear to reflect the kind of character that would accept compromise. Every person there was armed with handguns and all had rifles nearby stacked in an upright position. She did not see any children or young people in the group. These men and women were the leaders of the survivalist groups and they were experienced in warfare.

In a flat emotionless voice Charlene James said, "The earth and everyone on it are going to be destroyed by an alien entity not from our dimension or universe. The longest we have is maybe one generation before they arrive. However, those in charge now think the initial attacks will occur sooner, perhaps within a year. The exact time is unknown. I have been asked to approach you and to advise you of what is coming and ask you to assist in organizing a network for defense. Weapons and munitions will be provided by the government and another interested party."

Everyone sat in shocked silence. The young woman sitting next to Charlene James reached for the bottle of whisky and took a long swig.

Frank Morningstar said, "When can we meet these people and how will they supply us with weapons?"

Charlene James said, "I have a communication devise and if you allow them to come here to confirm what I have said is true, they will. If you are not interested and do not wish to be affiliated with them, they will go away and leave you alone in peace and find others willing to help. Whither you choose to join them or not you will end up fighting these being and you will all die."

"They only ask that I vouch for you in regards to their safety and they vouched to me as to your safety. Really, if they wanted to harm you or wanted us dead, we would already be dead. All other information you need to know should come from them. They are the ones that contacted me due to my expertise with survivalist groups and asked me to set up this meeting. What little I know of them indicates they are trustworthy. And as strange and as improbable as it is, the woman Commander in charge of earth security, and I, have mutual high school friends."

Again, everyone was silent. It was a bleak assessment. They were waiting for Frank Morningstar to make a decision.

Frank said, "Due to its unusual nature I think we all should be of one accord. If any of you do not wish to have a meeting with these people, whoever or whatever they are, you should say so. You may leave now and no one will find fault."

Everyone looked around but no one got up to leave.

"All those in favor of meeting them to hear what they have to say, raise your right hand."

Everyone raised their right hand.

Charlene James said, "I must warn you, the men

and women you are about to meet are called, Space Intelligence Special Forces. They all have been in many engagements. I tell you this not to scare you but to tell you to respect them, as they will respect you."

"The group is made up of Human and Andrians. Other than the Human members of the group, they originated on a planet named Andria, located in another galaxy. However, all of them have spent their entire lives aboard an Intergalactic Carrier. Perhaps some may have been on a planet before, but for most, Earth is their first "adventure".

"They are telepaths, thus they are mostly non-verbal. Their life skills are designed for survival, not small talk. Every one of them are willing to die for you if necessary."

Frank Morningstar looked at Charlene James and said, "This should be really interesting. Bring them in."

Charlene James raised her hand to her mouth and said, "You may land now."

CHAPTER 32
FLATA'S FEAR

Emily, Flata, and the accompanying Spiritual Angelic Beings entered thru the great wall entrance where they soon came to a gate which allowed entrance to a tunnel of light. Again, the Spiritual Beings around the glowing inner gate indicated for Emily to proceed as they themselves remained at the entrance to the tunnel. After exiting the tunnel of light Emily observed the alter with the golden chair and it was again unoccupied.

Emily, for the second time, heard the voice," Emily, come here."

As the voice said that she and Flata received a vision and was propelled out into the cosmos among the brilliant lights of fire and immersed in the burning of an untold number of stars.

The Supreme Being said, "This is my creation. It is a preparation for worlds to come. These worlds will be occupied by my spirit children, as you once were and then sent to occupy the earth. Except for you Flata. As you already know, your species is much older."

"Flata, your species was created in the primordial cauldron of the first star. The creation spread in the blink of an eye. Your specie was swept away into a different dimension lost among the nebula of a magnetic flux that diminished time and space to nothing but a spec, even smaller than the smallest quark. Then a magnificent ball of light of many colors burst into being and thrust your species world back into the proper dimension. Your spirit light, though dim, began to shine in the cosmos once again."

"Yours was not the only species lost among the firmament. There were others. Two such specie was found by you Emily. They were what you call the Mermaids and the Neanderthals. Both of their worlds were part of the initial creation. They too are exceedingly old creations. Your bravery and commitment helped saved them from extinction."

Emily responded, "Not I my Lord, but the Bio-Mechanical Entity within the saucers alerted me to the presence of the life forms as their distress calls echoed thru the cosmos. The bio-entity and I are now one. I joined with the entity to enable me to find a way to destroy the species from a different dimension. I have no understanding how it was possible to become one with the entity but the entity is much more knowledgeable than both the Andrians and Human species combined."

"And tell me Emily, from whence did this Intelligence, "Entity", as you call it, come?"

Emily could feel Flata beside her and she knew she was somewhat afraid to answer the Creator of the Universe. That was good. Perhaps her fear would instill some humility within her spirit.

Before Emily could answer, Flata said, "I did my Lord. I really do not know how it came about. I was experimenting with various compounds combined with our fusion generators. We needed help making our environment more habitable. As you know, we are a space faring specie and we must generate all our needs. As the lead genetics specialist for our group of five intergalactic carriers, I am responsible for all our lives. The decisions I make are life and death decisions. They are very hard. I was looking for some way to help mollify the laws of strict adherence to make our lives more…," looking at Emily smiling, "humane, if you will."

Emily squeezed her hand.

"I was born and raised on an inter-galactic carrier. One hundred percent of our energies and intelligence was devoted to survival. As Emily would say, there was no "fun" in our lives. We had no knowledge of our Creator until Emily was brought on board and she constantly prayed to you. A search of our history showed that at one time in the far echoes of our distant past there was references to a Great Creator. And yes, when Emily told me that my creation was alive and she could converse with it, I was elated beyond all measure and thought in that moment that I was God because I did create a sentient being from an inanimate object. Not only did the creation become self-aware but it was able to replicate the learning process. The Entity eventually became more intellectually advanced than ourselves. Had it not claimed Emily as its own, I would have considered destroying it."

"I believe this creation to be without a soul and thus perhaps the propensity to do evil would outweigh the desire to do good. However, since the Entity has become one with Emily, I believe her soul stands instead. I have had many sleepless nights dreading my worst fears would come true. It is in moments like these that I realize how foolish I was to even attempt such a creation and even much worse for me to exalt in and take pride in the feat. I ask your forgiveness for this blatant lack of humility."

There was silence for a long period of time as no one spoke; it seemed as if the heavens discontinued singing their song. Flata trembled beside Emily in fear and humility and Emily trembled in fear for Flata.

The Lord spoke, "You are forgiven for your hubris. I understand your need for higher guidance. It is true your specie appears to have been abandoned by the Spirit of Conscious Desire."

"My son was supposed to watch over you but he rebelled against me and was cast out after a long and prolonged war. Your specie was lost in the fog of war. As you have found a way to improve your specie, Human and Andrian, by sharing the building blocks of life, you will be exalted in the heavens to come. I will not allow the Evil One's creation to destroy all life in my universe. I will preserve you and create a new heaven and a new earth for in which you shall dwell. Emily, as for the Entity which dwells in you, I will bless you with the power of control over all such creations in this world and all worlds to come. Now quickly return to earth as the enemy comes."

When the Lord said these words, Emily found herself and Flata floating over the front porch of her house. All the children were looking up in amazement at her. None of them could speak as Flata floated back to her seat on the porch. Emily then returned to the Intergalactic Carrie to assist Blain and Sasha.

CHAPTER 33
TWO DAYS BEFORE INVASION COMING TO AGREEMENT

The group of survivalists stood in awe if not fear as they observed six saucer landing craft and one cigar shaped craft break thru the clouds near the ridge and gently land in the pasture before them about three hundred feet away. A ramp came down from the side of the saucer craft and several men and women exited the craft. The men and women formed up in a military formation in front of their crafts. A young woman about thirty, flanked by two older men and a strange looking tall, muscular, woman, with flaming red hair and who was topless exhibiting large breast, of all things, walked from the craft toward Frank Morningstar.

The young woman was indeed young, maybe thirty. When she was about ten feet away, she stood at attention and with an about face said, "Troops, attention! Salute!"

All the troops went to attention and executed a perfect salute.

The young woman then did another about face and saluted Frank Morningstar.

Frank Morningstar, along with the entire compliment,

stood at attention and returned the salute.

Sara said, "Two! At ease!"

Sara's troops went back into the saucers and began bringing down large long containers using levitating technology, and lined them up in long parallel rows.

Sara began by saying, "It is nice to meet you Sgt. Morningstar. I am Commander Sara Sears. This man is my father, Commander Caleb Sears, and this man is Commander Taaker. He is Andrian from the planet Andria in a Galaxy far away from the milky way galaxy. My father and Commander Taaker initially were to find alternative narratives when someone reported ufo,s and other strange anomalies. Now they will work directly with you and act as liaison between your group and our group, should you choose to work with us."

"And last but not least, this beautiful exotic woman is Muskula. She was and is the leader of the Sea Star People. She cannot speak but she is a skilled telepath."

Muskula looked over the crowd and was not surprised to find most men and some women staring at her breast.

"Hello."

Everyone was startled because they heard her in their head, a new experience for them.

"I was the leader of the Sea Star People. We were a water world specie and numbered as the sands of the oceans in which we lived. The enemy flowed from the sky into the waters and came in never ending numbers. We fought them killing untold millions of them but there was always more. There was twenty-six of us left fighting when we were rescued by Emily Smith and a living intelligence within her saucer and other Human and Andrian Space Intelligence Special Forces. Had it not been for them our entire specie would have been destroyed. I am now the commander of Earths Ocean Forces."

Everyone was stunned silent as Sara was hoping they would be. They were in shock. That too was good, it helped her gain the advantage.

"Frank Morningstar, you have quiet an impressive service record which includes the silver star, not to mention the many purple hearts. Your name was the only name I required of Charlene James before meeting with your group. I used you as a gage as to the caliber of people with whom you choose to serve and I was to meet. We are all impressed."

Frank Morningstar looked closely at the young woman. She had obviously been in combat as part of her ear was missing and she had fine lines like knife wounds across her cheeks. He did not recognize any of the uniforms and insignias but assumed they were Space Intelligence Commandoes as the woman Muskula had said. In addition to her sidearm she had two knives strapped to her calves

"Okay, I am impressed. Is it true that an alien entity is coming to destroy the earth and everyone on it? You want to have an alliance for what? We cannot save the earth so what is the point of forming an alliance and fighting?"

Sara said, "You are correct. What we told Charlene James is true. We cannot defeat an enemy that has a never-ending supply of soldiers and is willing to sacrifice untold numbers to destroy us. We are the only specie that has ever been able to stand up to them. They have already destroyed an unknown number of worlds and every sentient lifeform upon them."

"We, mainly the Andrians, have fought them across many galaxies trying to save as many worlds as possible but without success. But since we stood against them, they are bypassing all other worlds and are coming directly to earth. There is an unknown number of Inter-Galactic Carriers, battle ships if you will, currently fighting them to impede their progress. Because of the nature of this enemy, the children have been removed, they currently live here on earth."

"Three of these carriers with five thousand souls on each carrier has been destroyed. Once they are able to time warp onto their target, we are unable to dislodge them and they board until the crew is over-whelmed. It does not matter how many of them are killed. "

"We have secretly been evaluating and selecting young people for the past ten years to be placed on arks and sent into unknown directions in space to help save our specie. The candidates are selected based upon their mathematical and scientific skills. That is what they are going to need to be a space faring society and increase their chance of survival. The first ship was launched yesterday. There were fifty thousand souls. We basically abducted them. They had no knowledge of the program. They are in suspended animation and will be so for at least a hundred years. When they wake up, the earth and everyone on it will be destroyed. Also, stored on the ship is a DNA data bank of as many Humans and Andrians as we could possibly collect. That program too has been on going ten years."

"We no longer believe we have a generation for the enemy to arrive. We believe their arrival, of at least an advanced group, is imminent. In all probability it will be an intelligence gathering mission to see how we respond. We will not under any circumstances allow any of them to escape. They will all die. They do not take prisoners. We fight them until either, one of us or both of us are dead. We have no choice. The only alternative is to surrender and be killed."

"So, Mr. Morningstar, the answer to your question as to why fight if there is no chance of winning? I for one intend to take as many of those life forms with me as I can. All the Space Intelligence Commandoes, U.S. Military, and many, many other associates feel the same way. The question is, are you in or are you out?"

Frank Morningstar looked around at the men and women gathered in his group. They all looked resolute.

"Okay guys. It is up to you. Shall we join them?"

Everyone raised their hand.

Sara approached Frank Morningstar and said, "Raise your right hand. Anyone under my command must take an oath. The Oath is yours and their bond to me. Break the oath and you die, by my hand."

Frank Morningstar looked the woman named Sara in the eye. As a warrior he had no problem discerning the look in her eye and was aware that it connected to her heart. He also knew that in all probability she could and would kill him should he break the oath.

After Frank had taken the oath, Sara said, "You now hold the rank of Commander and you are in charge of all of Earths civilian resistance forces. Your liaison with headquarters will be Commanders Sears and Taaker. All the men and women in my command are here to train you with your new weapons. Before we start it is necessary to show you holo vids of our enemy so you may know we speak the truth."

Charlene James had not realized it but she had moved closer to Frank Morningstar and had taken his hand in hers. He responded with a soft pressure which later became a tight grip. As they all watched a holo vid of the alien enemy boarding and killing every living crew member on board an Intergalactic Carrier and then overcoming and destroying a whole planet; they all cried out with one accord, some falling to their knees calling out to God to save them. Sara understood their despair. She too had called out to God many times.

"Oh, one other thing, this is an excellent camp for hiding from the government, or my father if you will; he was assigned to the anti- terrorist unit before he was recruited by Emily Smith to cover for aliens.", Sara said with a sweet smile on her face looking at her Father.

"However, it is basically a tomb for fighting with this alien enemy. The enemy will fill the area with an acid mist which will sink to the lowest level. You cannot escape. Your best position for a standoff defense will be on high ground, have plenty of room to maneuver, and then make them come to you. I assure you they will be eager to please."

Frank Morningstar looked closely at the tall rugged blonde-haired man. He did look familiar but from when or where he could not recall.

Commander Sears walked over to Frank Morningstar and shook his hand saying, "You may not recall where you know me from but you were the one that saved my life one night after I became engaged in a fist fight with some of your sentries." I had infiltrated your group and had made an assessment that you and your group was not a threat to the government. I was trying to sneak away and was caught by your sentries. They proceeded to beat me up and you intervened. I told you my wife was pregnant and I had to leave. You allowed me to do so."

Commander Morningstar smiled saying, "Yes, I remember now. If I recall they were getting ready to shoot you in the head. It is a small world."

Sara then said, "Well Commander, it shows boys will be boys. Now you need to choose two individuals to be second and third in command. They shall be your captains. Every one of you here will be sworn into the Space Intelligence and receive a commission. Each of you will be required to develop your own command to serve in different parts of the country. You can all train and use the weapons provided. But for now, I would like for you, Commander Morningstar, and your two chosen advisors, along with Charlene James, to accompany us back to base. You need to understand the magnitude of effort being put forth to protect the earth. Also, all these individuals here, the ones you have chosen, will be given a ride in a saucer at some point in time should any of you wish to do so. We will fly you to the moon and get you up close and personal with an Intergalactic Carrier."

"If you all would accompany me, we will return to base."

CHAPTER 34
DESPERATE MEASURES

Blain and Sasha was on the bridge when an alarm sounded. There was no indication of any kind of imminent incursion so the alarm took them by surprise. The deck tilted to the side as the Captain of the Intergalactic Carrier shifted direction contrary to the laws of physics. When they discussed with the Captain how he managed to keep the alien enemy from overwhelming the ship and break their previous interspatial incursion onto the ship he advised that since all was lost, it called for a desperate maneuver.

The Intergalactic Carrier was not designed to reverse direction while in a magnetic wave. However, the reversal worked and the interspatial incursion was blocked by the magnetic wave.

The inter-ship communication sounded throughout the ship. "Stand by to repel boarders! Ship has been boarded! Breach is in the bionic gardens on deck seven!"

The announcement "Stand by to repel borders", was the same warning handed down through the centuries on all ships at sea and now in space. It appeared the warning was also adopted and applied to the Andrians as well but before this enemy, no one had ever boarded an Andrian vessel without being brought on board for experiments or invited as the Humans were when they were looking for Emily Smith who had been abducted by Blain. They had brashly gone to the Intergalactic carrier and literally knocked on their "door".

Blain and Sasha quickly donned their acid resistant combat suits and ran to the location given for the incursion. They were joined by numerous other special forces members.

As they entered the ten-acre forested enclosure, Blain saw a steady stream of alien life forms falling from a shimmering circle from the overhead. They flowed like mud in every direction. The enemy was quickly filling up the enclosure with acid to aid in their communications. Blain used a synthetic molecular lightening beam to cut through the fog of acid. He then focused the beam onto the ever-increasing flow of aliens from the circular shimmer in the overhead. Many of them fell dead on the deck. All the plants and trees within the enclosure were already dead having been exposed to the highly caustic acid.

The beam did little to inhibit their communication but it did help to cause confusion among the enemy. Other members, using the same weapon, joined the battle. Using lasers tuned to the enemy's body mass, an untold number of them were destroyed. Their bodies were beginning to pile up to over twenty feet high in the center of the ten acre enclosure. Of course, body count was a moot point if the Captain could not break the inter-spatial time warp lock. The enemy never ran out of bodies.

Again, the Carrier lunged, seemingly in two directions at the same time. Everyone lost traction as the gravity assist units went out of sync with the movements of the carrier. And suddenly, just as it appeared, the shimmering circle of the time warp disappeared and the flow of enemy aliens ceased to flow from the overhead.

Gravity assist was again restored and Sasha and Blain led a charge toward the remaining aliens firing their weapons and neutralizing their communications. Soon every enemy combatant was dead. The death toll on the ship's personnel was limited to the workers within the bionic garden compound. There was about seventy men and women that died a very painful and gruesome death.

As robots entered the enclosure and began filtering the air and expelling it out into space, the bodies of the enemy aliens were loaded into containers and they too were consigned to the cold depths of space. Specialized robots neutralized the acid in the soil and removed the dead plants and sterile soil. Thus, the production process of these resources somewhat diminished the amount of oxygen available for breathing on the carrier. Because of this, an asteroid was taken in traction and the chemical components were broken down to obtain the oxygen and water. Other parts of the asteroid were ground down to a fine soil. Nutrients were added and plants were re-established which grew rapidly with growth hormone technology.

Sasha and Blain met the Captain on the bridge. Everyone was stoic just believing that perhaps their next breath would be their last. The Andrian attention to detail in the face of death was phenomenal. It was not so much so with the human complement of the crew but their professionalism and training in the face of danger carried them thru the crises. Sasha was proud of her unit. They had proven themselves time and again in the face of imminent death. They took pride in showing themselves as equal to their Andrian counterparts.

Blain, Sasha, and the Captain enclosed themselves in their battle cocoons to share information they got from Emily on her first visit. It was a relief to know that Sara was doing such a good job. Defending the earth and the family was a tremendous undertaking. They were sure that Flata had done something to enhance her mental skills and capabilities to help in this task.

Evidently it was true that Emily had met with the Supreme Being and was enlightened as to what was to come. That was to be the subject which Blain and Sasha wanted to discuss with the Captain.

Blain started the discussion. Even though they once again had avoided imminent death due to the Captains' skills they knew it was only a matter of time before they would not be so lucky. It appeared the enemy knew they were the command ship and had targeted their Carrier more than any other. Their primary military objective was to stay alive and slow the enemy advance toward earth.

Blain said, "Emily told us that we cannot defeat our enemy because there was just too many of them and they were designed by an evil Supreme Being. She said our focus was to stay alive as long as possible and stall the enemy from reaching Earth to give Sara and the others time to remove as many selectees as they could before the Earth would be destroyed. She also said it was in our Supreme Being's Plan that the enemy should arrive at the earth at which time, "The Point of No Time", will have been reached. At that designated time the enemy will be cast into a different dimension consisting of a great void."

The Captain looked at Blain steadily gauging what he had been told and weighing the possibilities of outlasting the enemy's ability to gain access to the Carrier all the way across the galactic void to earth.

The Captain said, "How can we continue to battle them across the void with diminishing resources. We have to come up with a battle plan that will distract their advance and make them look elsewhere other than the earth."

"We have located several of their command ships, perhaps we can board their vessels and conduct diversion type tactics. They obviously are intelligent and follow command instructions. Since we do not have enough black hole generators to stop them and soon not even slow their advances then we must try something new. I suggest small raiding parties to different parts of their ship."

Blain responded," In all probability they would be suicide missions. There is nothing wrong with a suicide mission as long as the reward is exponentially hundreds of times greater than the sacrifice."

Sasha, always thinking said, "And we know they have more than one command ship. If we could knock out several at once, it may take more time for them to reorganize. We have sent intelligence gathering vehicles among them several times and they have completely ignored them. Perhaps it was due to their size and they felt they were no threat."

"True, we may not even have to board. We just have to open them like a can opener and expose them to space. They have probably moved their command ships to the middle of the group to lessen the likely hood of being sucked into one of our generated black holes."

"Sasha, when you think outside the parameters of accepted military tactics you go way out! I should not forget it was your tactics that captured and demoralized our Andrian traitors in the desert. It was ingenious to extract them from the desert area at the end of a rope attached to a large balloon, which was snatched by one of your old airplanes! It was humiliating to us and by a woman of all things!" The Captain smiled and just shook his head.

Looking at Sasha with a grin on his face, Blain said, "I like your style"!

The captain looked on smiling. Of course, everyone in the entire fleet had heard of and seen the video of the extraction of the Andrian landing party and the story had become legendary as had Sasha's reputation as a warrior. "Please remind me Commander Sasha to never get on your bad side!"

They all laughed. It was a stress reliever and good to clear their mind for planning the new tactics.

CHAPTER 35
UNPLANNED BAPTISM OF FIRE (INVASION DAY)

Frank Morningstar and Charlene James followed Sara to the largest saucer that was toward the back of the group. As they passed saucers being unloaded, the newly Commissioned Commander Morningstar observed numerous crates packed into several saucers still to be unloaded. Like a kid at Christmas, he was torn between wanting to stay and see what was in the crates or see and experience the new wonders promised by what he had visually before him, an actual flying saucer.

Sara walked up the ramp of her command saucer which was three times as large as the supply saucers; holding hands, Morningstar and Charlene James followed. Holding hands just seemed like such a natural thing to do. At the top of the ramp they hesitantly looked in at the darkened interior with muted red light. The area was filled with tube like structures and if they were for troops the ship would easily hold up to a hundred personnel. They did not realize this command saucer consisted of three decks.

Sara stopped in front of a chair like device suspended

by cables and electrical wiring, somewhat lower than the deck on which they were standing. Turning and facing them, Sara took Frank Morningstar by the biceps and slowly pressured him into one of the tubes. Charlene James followed suit without any coxing. So did the two selected Captains.

Sara advised, "A tube will come from above and seal you in to equalize the pressure. A small tube and bladder will cover your mouth and nose and will provide you oxygen. And, since I want you awake, I will not render you unconscious."

Sara smiled when she looked at Charlene James.

"We will take a short tour of our moon facilities but we will not land. There are five Intergalactic Carriers docked there for maintenance. Half of the personnel are in our earth base and half remain in the Carriers in the event of an emergency, thus our base remains fairly crowded."

"The base population has an extra twelve thousand personnel. Also, none of them have had the extra finger added to fit in to our society so do not be surprised. And like I said earlier, they are all telepaths and not inclined for small talk. So, do not be offended if they ignore you or do not reply to a solicitous and friendly hello. Actually, they are apprehensive being on a planet as there is nothing between them and the atmosphere."

After her personal guard consisting of ten men and women had taken their place within their individual tubes, along with the tall Muskular woman that was a mermaid, Sara assumed her position and was quickly cocooned within her command chair. Immediately Sara began to emit a soft green glow which surrounded her countenance and it appeared that she fell into a trance.

The forward bulkhead shimmered and became opaque allowing one to see outside. Frank Morningstar watched the camp slowly recede as the saucer lifted from the encampment. There was another short vibration and again the bulkhead shimmered as the curvature of the earth far below came into view. There was one more short vibration and the saucer appeared to be suspended in the blackness of space with an untold number of diamonds and galaxies shining in the distance.

Sara allowed the Saucer to float and turn slowly. An up close and personal view of the moon came into view. Sara guided the saucer to the far side of the moon where the five Intergalactic Carriers and many other craft of all sizes and description busily moved between enormous constructs of which served an indeterminant number of functions. The surface of the moon looked more like a large city with buildings extending from one side of the moon terrain to the other. It certainly was not pristine and virgin undisturbed soil like the side facing the earth.

Sara floated over the far side for about two hours as she allowed her guest to view the elaborate defenses, buildings and Inter Galactic Carriers and then returned to base. She could read her new commanders mind and was sure it was set in stone in his desire to organize Earth's forces. Charlene James, having been sworn into Space Intelligence as the leading Information Officer for dissemination of information on the earth, was also committed heart and soul in her duties. She held the rank of Captain.

The landing inside the base was as awe inspiring as the trip around the moon. The facility had now been expanded to take up all the space within the mountain. The number of saucers lined up to a distance of five miles. There were other smaller craft and intelligence gathering devices just as numerous.

Upon Sara exiting the craft there was over five hundred Space Intelligence Special Forces lined up in formation on either side of the walk way. Frank James, always the warrior, recognized not only the commitment, respect, and professionalism of the military unit but he could, for some unknown reason, feel what appeared to be love, extended to Commander, Sara Sears.

Sara stopped at the top of the ramp, she placed her hands crossing over her heart looking to the left and then to the right. Using telepathy Sara said, "I am humbled to serve as your Commander. I will not ever ask you to take any assignment that I would not take myself."

"I will now share with you, information that I received from our Commander, Emily Smith, and you should share with others. Emily has become one with the biomechanical Entity that was within her saucer and thus she is no longer a corporal being. Exactly what she is or what her status is, we do not know."

"Emily said that what is happening is according to a divine plan. We were chosen to lure this enemy to the earth and then delay the inevitable. What is the inevitable?"

Sara paused for effect. It was the most singularly, salient, point, for all mankind. "The earth and everyone on it, every plant, insect, and animal will be destroyed."

Frank Morningstar and Charlene James saw every head jerk compulsively toward Sara. They did not hear what she said but they could figure out pretty much the content.

Sara quickly explained the new revelation of, "The Point of No Time".

"It is that point in time which encompasses the translation of those of us that are alive at that moment and are called to serve in a future capacity. The others that are alive at that time and not called to serve will be instantly changed to spiritual beings, as will those individuals that are resurrected from their graves and receive their spiritual bodies; all of which is a mystery to everyone regardless of their spirituality."

She talked about the New Heaven and the New Earth. And what role they would play in it, whither one was a resurrected being or a translated being. She used the examples in the scriptures referencing the individuals that did not die but were taken for a specific purpose to be used at a later time such as Enoch, Elijah, and Moses; Elijah and Moses being the most recognizable due to their appearance with Jesus on the Mount during the Transfiguration of Christ, of which Peter, James, and John was also present and they too were transfigured.

"It was obvious that Elijah and Moses were translated because, it was prior to the resurrection of Christ, and especially for Elijah because he was taken up in a whirlwind. And, none of the individuals had ever died. Scriptures say that Jesus was the "First Fruits", therefore they were translated beings that remained in the corporeal state and had mortal bodies. This may call into question about the resurrection of Lazarus among others. They were resurrected as mortal beings and would taste physical death again at a later point in time. The translated beings will not die but at a later time they will be changed into spiritual beings when they have completed whatever task they were called to do."

All the hybrid children will be translated. They will be the leaders of those of us that are also translated and will be given work to do in the new heavens and new earth. I know for sure that one of our task will be to locate the seed ships and bring them to a proposed coordinates, of a new earth, of which there will be many, where we will be their teachers and protectors.

Sara also told them what was in store for the evil beings from the different dimension that did not remain in their place. It would not go well for them.

She further informed them that Commanders Sasha and Blain, on the Intergalactic Carriers, stated they had been boarded twice but the Captain was able to break the spatial time warp. And since they are getting low on fire power, they are going to start boarding assaults on the enemy's command ships in an effort to continue to slow them down.

"They are doing their part and we must do our part, and that is, when the enemy arrives it is our duty to kill as many of them as possible and further delay them until, "The Point of No Time", has been reached. That is our mission and our calling. Dismissed."

TARGET EARTH

The special forces group broke rank in silence each carrying their own thoughts. It appeared the end was near.

Sara escorted Frank Morningstar and Charlene James and the two Captains into the armory and showed them the various weapons which was to be available to them but by no means all there was available.

"Charlene James, I know you do not consider yourself a soldier or a warrior but the truth is, if you are to die, would you not prefer die fighting? Therefore, you also need to be suited with an acid resistant armor suit and take weapons training, starting today. At least you need to learn to point and shoot. Believe me, the enemy will be so thick you cannot miss."

Charlene James felt a cold shiver go thru her body and unbidden beads of sweat moistened her back.

Charlene James and Frank Morningstar along with his two advisers were fitted with the new acid resistant suits and then Sara took them to the firing range area and she made a special effort to teach Charlene James the rudimentary skills of using the laser look and shoot system. Sara felt like he owed it to their mutual friends, Haley and Kyla, especially to Haley. Haley had died a senseless death at the hands of her boyfriend. She did not even have a chance to graduate high school.

Sara left them practicing which they did for several hours and she herself went to the control and command center. As she reached for her coffee, she heard the unmistakable alarm indicating that an attack was underway.

Sara ran to her command saucer along with more

than a thousand special forces. She saw Charlene James and Frank Morningstar running up the ramp of her saucer and quickly take their places among the other men and women that were assigned to Sara's unit.

Sara jumped into the command chair and was immediately ensconced within the command cocoon.

Charlene James could not grasp the time differential between taking off and landing, it seemed like a dream frame from one point to the next. She had no more than taken a breath and the ramp door opened to the outside. Everyone ran out of the saucer in a rushed orderly manner, Charlene James and Frank Morningstar moved accordingly.

Upon exiting the saucer onto the sand, she ran toward the water and it was just as Sara had said it would be, she did not need to aim, she just pointed and fired. The beings were so ugly and disgusting and extremely terrifying. She fired her laser continuously and still the ugly things emerged from the water. She did not know how many she killed. Again, just as Sara had said, body count was immaterial.

The attack point was a ten-miles long stretch of the beach. The area was littered with the alien entities, bodies sliced into many pieces. There was also a large number of civilian casualties as their bare bones littered the beach water front.

Charlene James saw Sara race down the beach toward a woman and two children. Sara dove in front of the woman just as the alien entity fired a steady stream of acid. The acid struck Sara squarely in the chest as Sara fired her laser cutting the alien into many pieces. Immediately five Space Commandoes picked Sara up and carried her back to the saucer. A robotic drone dropped a net over the woman and the two children and threw them toward the saucer where another drone caught them and deposited them at the saucer entrance.

Sara was placed into a levitating medical drone and carried into the saucer which immediately took off. It did not take long after Sara's evacuation before the alien entities stopped coming out of the water. Soon after the last alien exited the water and was destroyed, a large contingent of mermaids exited the ocean led by the large woman Charlene James had met earlier.

She was fierce looking in her battle armor and her face appeared to be set in stone and was surrounded by flaming red hair that took on a life of its own. She was beautiful and appeared to be something that only Hollywood could envision. A large man standing next to her was just as striking and he appeared to be chiseled from granite. Their weapons were long lances with tips glowing a dull azure blue.

Charlene James and Frank Morningstar returned to the area where they had disembarked the saucer which had since departed with Sara. The woman and two children which had been literally snatched from the jaws of death by Sara's self-sacrifice was standing on the beach clutching the two children close to her body.

As Charlene James got closer to her she recognized her child hood friend Kyla.

"Kyla? Kyla! How amazing it is to see you and under

such an extremely unlikely set of circumstances!

Kyla, upon hearing her name called out turned toward the familiar voice which she could not quiet place. She saw a young woman her age in a military combat uniform. Improbable as it seemed, she saw her childhood friend from long ago whom she had lost contact with upon graduation from high school.

"Charlene James! Yes! How improbable to see you under such dreadful circumstances! You are absolutely the last person I would have envisioned as having joined the military. I read your columns every chance I get. I thought you were researching survivalist groups."

It was then that Kyla notices the large Native American male standing behind her, he too was also in uniform. He looked every inch the warrior.

"Kyla, I would like to introduce you to Frank Morningstar. He is the new commander of civilian resistance forces in our country. I am his assistant in helping to organize civilian resistance forces and I am also the liaison between the civilian forces and the military forces. But enough for old time sake, we need to go see how Sara is doing."

Frank Morningstar said, "You go ahead, I will stay here and assist any way possible. I will see you at the base camp. Oh, and by the way, you handled yourself nicely. You can watch my back anytime."

With that, Frank Morningstar turned and trotted down the beach to help other military units clear the area of the dead alien entities.

Charlene James burst with pride, her cheeks reddening

to a crimson. She did not expect any kind of compliment but the part about having his back really pleased her. It was at this time she started shaking as the adrenalin in her system begged for release. The two women hugged each other shivering in the heat of the sun, and arm in arm walked toward a saucer. The two children going before them proceeding up the saucer ramp wide-eyed realizing just how close they all came to death. Neither was allowed to turn around and look at the beach which was littered with those that were not as fortunate.

As they were going up the ramp Kyla was alert and observant as she now knew what all the hard work was about. It was then that Kyla again thought of Sara and how she had saved her and her children's lives.

"Let's go find Sara and see if she is okay."

Several of the Space Marines followed them up the ramp and assisted Kyla and the children into the tube. As the saucer gained altitude the wall became opaque and the beach became visible. The area was littered with the corpses of the dead, human and alien.

CAPTER 36
PRAYERS UNCEASING

Charlene James and Kyla parted ways upon landing in the hanger. All the space commandoes moved to a decontamination area to have the acid residue removed from their uniforms. Waves of ultraviolet light washed over the uniformed troops causing the molecules of acid to release and be sucked into a disposal system.

After storing her uniform in her newly acquired locker Charlene James donned a coverall uniform which already had name stenciled above the left breast pocket. Thinking that if anything, the military was sure efficient.

The news of Sara's heroic save of her friend Kyla had already spread thru the ranks of the troops, as did the news of her combat injury. The conversations were muted as an untold number of silent prayers were sent into the ether.

Charlene James was escorted to the emergency hospital into the waiting room. There was a large number of young people present. They were all reassuring a young man named Jawane that Sara was going to be fine as their Grandma Flata was tending to her.

"Jawane, you know that Grandma Flata is a miracle worker. Sara is going to be fine. If she can cure me of terminal brain cancer snatching me from the jaws of death just weeks before my supposed demise to be, she can repair any damage from the acid burns of these alien abominations."

The declaration was spoken by a young woman. She was reed thin, had long stringy blonde hair, and was a spitting image of an iconic flower child of a century gone by. This was only reinforced by her guitar laying on the table in front of the couch. It too had a look that perhaps it came from a museum.

Charlene James walked over to Kyla and sat next to her saying, "Who is the young girl?"

Kyla said, "I do not know. She is obviously part of the family. The young man Sara's age is Jawane. From what I have heard they have known each other since his arrival from where ever they are from. They were twelve years old."

"We were contacted by Sara's father and another man and were recruited to do legal procurement contracts. Sara would come in from time to time to check on progress and Jawane would usually be with her. As for who they are and where they are from you are privier to that information than I. I knew something strange was up I just could not put the pieces together."

Everyone sat in the waiting room and the only thing heard was muted conversations. Kyla's two children, Haley and Paul, were seated quietly not speaking. They too were still trying to process what happened.

Charlene James said, "I cannot stay long, I hope Sara is going to be okay. I need to prepare statements as to what happened on the beach today. I do not know how the military can possibly hide such a large-scale event that occurred in broad daylight. I need to come up with a cover story. There had to be at least over one thousand people on the beach, half of whom met a dreadful death."

Kyla thought for a minute and then said, "What about a large explosion of a military vessel filled with a chemical warfare agent that causes death and delusions? The survivors can be somehow induced to believe the alien creatures was part of the delusion?"

Charlene James looked at Kyla in amazement.

"Kyla! That is amazing! I think you should have my job. You came up with that so quick. I did not even know where to start."

An extremely handsome man about forty or so came into the room. He was accompanied by a very beautiful woman. Immediately a young teenager who was evidently the boyfriend of the throwback hippie girl and the couple's son, ran to his father and hugged him.

"Sara has been injured and is having an operation. We think she will be okay."

Warren hugged his son and said, "What happened to her?"

There was a momentary silence in the room as the group had not yet come up with a plausible explanation.

Before any one said anything Charlene James jumped up and walking over to the couple said, "There was an accident right off the coast of the beach this afternoon. A navy vessel carrying a large quantity of chemical warfare agents on board blew up killing the entire crew and the chemicals were spewed onto the beach killing an untold number of beach goers. The chemicals were acid base and those directly affected died quickly and painlessly. Others that breathed in the gas experienced hallucinations and are being tended to by military medical personnel."

She then stuck out her hand and said, "Charlene James. I am the information officer attached to the military and am responsible for dispensing information relating to military operations. In this case, a real tragedy.

Warren shook her hand wondering why she was at the hospital and not at work. Warren Jr. reading his mind and was aware of the relationship between the woman named Charlene James, and Kyla and Sara.

"Dad, Charlene James is a mutual friend of Kyla and Haley, all of the them having gone to school together with Sara. I imagine she is just here to support her friend Kyla.

Charlene James responded, "Yes, thank you. I am here to support my friend Kyla. As soon as we find out that Sara is ok, I will most certainly have to go to work".

Upon that declaration she returned to her seat and took out her communication device provided to her by Sara earlier and sent the quick cover story to the military office. Soon the information would be disseminated among all branches of the military and personnel involved in the cleanup. She would need to return to the beach for a civilian broadcast to ensure the population remains calm and hopefully ignorant. The attack was too premature. From what she heard from the military chatter on the saucer, they all believed the attack was more of an intelligence gathering mission with the main attack yet to come sometime in the future.

The operation took longer than expected. About two hours had passed when an older woman came to the waiting room. She looked haggard.

"Children, Sara is going to be fine. You can all go in but not at the same time. Jawane, Sara has asked for you first so you should go on in."

Jawane turned without a word and entered thru the closed doors accessing the recovery area.

Flata looked over and saw Kyla standing to the side with another woman. Walking over to them Flata said, "Kyla, I understand Sara took the acid shot meant for you. You are very fortunate, as is she, for having killed the creature quick as she did. Had she not done so the encounter would have ended in a much different scenario."

A voice behind Flata said, "What do you mean Sara took an acid shot from a creature. We were told that a navy ship with a chemical agent blew up."

Flata turned around and saw Warren staring at her. She had not seen him in the crowd of children and military personnel. Indeed, how did he even get into the military hospital?

Flata said, "Be at peace Warren. All is well. You, misunderstood. There was a tremendous explosion on a navy ship right off the coast of the beach. All the navy personnel were killed. The explosion released all the chemical weapons of acid and gas which killed many people on the beach. The gas also causes extreme hallucinations which affected all the people that did not die."

Warrens eyes became distant as he softly repeated the mantra which was told to him by Flata.

TARGET EARTH

Charlene James looked on in amazement. Had she not seen and participated in the attack herself she too would have fell under Flata's spell.

Charlene James turned and hugged Kyla saying she had to go. Kyla gave her a business card and said, "Keep in touch and call me soon."

CHAPTER 37
COUNTER ATTACK IN THE VOID OF SPACE

Sasha and Blain met with the hundred commanders of the Intergalactic Carriers spread across the void between the stars with the Milky Way Galaxy and Earth behind them. The fleet had identified and targeted the command ships of the alien intruders and had successfully obliterated them from existence with black hole detonators. However, like the number of aliens killed on planets everywhere were replenished, so too were the command ships. Each and every time a command ship was destroyed, their whole fleet would stop for a significant period of time until a new command ship would emerge as command and control. Blain and Sasha could have taken out other command ships while their fleet was still but they believed more disruption could be achieved by allowing them time to regroup, give them the opportunity to move a short distance, and then take out another command ship

The enemy did not seem to mind the disruptions and their actions of stopping and delaying their advance seemed almost like their plan of attack.

Blain addressed the hundred commanders of the Intergalactic Carriers via the established neural net, each within their cocoon.

"Is it possible that we are missing something? Why do they not hurry? They act like they have all the time in the universe."

Sasha replied," Perhaps they are aware of, "The Point Of No Time". And if they are, they want to delay their inevitable demise?"

Another Commander spoke up, "What if there are two enemy fleets? Or even three?"

The discussion between the Commanders went on for an hour or more with each Commander adding a bit more to the supposition as to why the enemy seemed to delay. Nothing was resolved. The possible threat of a second or third fleet hung in the emptiness of space between them like a radiating neutron star. Many of the Captains believed they were just occupying the fleets attention while the enemy made an end run. They were right, they just did not know it.

Sasha said, "I will lead the first attack group and it will consist of over six hundred missile starlight interceptors. Each ship will carry only three crew. Our crews are not expendable. The primary objective will be to enter their ships, locate the troop storage areas and destroy them with shoulder fired neutron missiles. If we can burn them while they are in stasis, we should be able to eliminate them as a threat to our carriers."

"Drones and robots will be used to increase fire power and coverage within their ships. At least one AI drone will be dispatched to the bridge area of each boarded vessel, and if at all possible, the neural network should be destroyed. We will try this as a onetime option. After our invasion force returns safely, we will again counsel as to what our options are.

Sasha was ready and properly dressed in her combat uniform consisting of an acid resistant outer garment. Looking at Blain she said, "I feel good that we are doing something to eliminate some of our enemy. I know that this tactic is risky but what else are we to do? I have this feeling that we are missing key elements of their battle strategy. We are fighting in the blind as we have no actionable intelligence."

Blain took Sasha in his arms and kissed her long on the lips. "We are doing the best we can with what we have. At least they have been unable to board our carrier. Be lean, mean, and smart. Come back to me. We will devise a new strategy upon your return after assessing the effectiveness of our offensive. This should catch them totally by surprise as we have never ventured an attack outside of our carriers."

Sasha kissed Blain once more and said, "See you when I see you". Sasha turned and boarded her fighter with her two crew. They launched with the other fighters at the appointed time.

As the small flotilla of fighters left the relative safety of the carriers they were enfolded in the blackness of space. The only visible light was the myriad of stars that glowed like beacons in the night. The carriers were far enough apart from one another that they were not visible to the naked eye. It appeared to be a lonely excursion and indeed it was as each fighter was on its own.

TARGET EARTH

It took several hours of travel at near light speed for Sasha's fighter to reach their target in the relative mist of their enemy. The alien craft loomed like a monstrous blob of mud literally a hundred miles wide. Sasha maneuvered her craft to the entrance portal of the space craft. Fortunately for them they had been gathering intelligence on the enemy alien space craft using AI robots and drones since first contact with their fleet. They enemy ignored them as they mapped out every nook and cranny of their vessels. It appeared that they believed they were impenetrable.

Sasha placed her fighter in front of the entrance portal and the AI system on board sent signals to the entry lock. It did not take long for the portal to open. Entering the enemy ship, the AI systems mapped the most logical route to what they believed to be the cryo storage area of the crew.

The fighter glided to a halt over what appeared to be a cavern a mile wide with a depth that curved out of view. The center area was criss- crossed with a myriad structure of beams. The walls were filled with what appeared to be small, square enclosures that contained the bodies of the enemy which were in stasis waiting to be summoned to do battle. The walls of containers had small access paths showing numerous square containers receding into the narrow paths into the soft red glow of some kind of light.

Sasha checked her surveillance monitors noting that the drones had reached the command and control center of the enemy vessel. The large area was saturated with a mist of acid which was used to communicate with other crew members within the ship and other ships within the fleet.

Sasha spoke a command and she observed several spherical balls enter into the enclosure disappearing within the mist of acid. Within seconds there was a burst of ultraviolet light that neutralized the acid mist ceasing all communication within the command center. Then there was a brilliant explosion as phosphorous gelatin as it splayed across the huge command center burning the occupants to a crisp.

Sasha smiled at the ease of nullifying the alien command and control center. "Launch the neutron missiles! Then our good fighter, get us out of here!"

A fleet of smart missiles quickly went to their appointed coordinates and waited until their appointed time to explode. Just as they arrived it appeared a beehive of activity began as the apertures containing the enemy alien soldiers flew open and an innumerable host of soldiers exited and began attacking the neutron bombs.

Sasha activated the emergency retreat and the fighter retraced it's path to the exit. As they approached the exit a wall of enemy soldiers filled the exit.

"Hold on!"

Sasha fired a small sonic missile controlled by AI. The missile entered their mist and immediately the wall began to vibrate and disintegrate as body parts became a jellied mass of matter which only moments before consisted of a whole being.

The fighter exited the portal.

"Close the entrance! Seal the portal!"

TARGET EARTH

Sasha and her two crew manned their weapons and started sweeping space with laser waves as the enemy began exiting the craft thru multiple access ports. Evidently the carrier had defensive soldiers on standby. At least they were not stupid, asleep perhaps.

At that moment the neutron bombs exploded making body material and DNA a jellied mass which was incinerated to a crisp. Every living being within the ship was eliminated from the universe. The alien soldiers exiting the craft lost their direction and they too would soon find themselves frozen in space, swept along by the magnetic pull of their space ship.

As Sasha and her crew docked in the hold of their Intergalactic Carrier they were met by Blain. He was worried as they were the last ship to return. All the fighter craft sent out returned safely with their missions accomplished. As for the enemy's response, the entire fleet once again halted and regrouped. They were not in any hurry.

All the commanders of the fleet again met in conference and discussed the enemy's reaction to the attack. It was not normal. They all came to the same conclusion, there had to be another enemy fleet approaching earth from a different quadrant.

Blain advised, "It is obviously time for us to return to earth. Hopefully we will get there in time to offer a defense. I think at least seventy percent of the fleet should return to earth now, those of us remaining will continue the fight here."

Blain dispatched the designated carriers of the fleet to return to the earth and for them to go at light speed.

Even light speed would not be enough to get there in time. They would have to engage the gravitation wave generators and fold time and space and go thru a few wormholes to get there in a timely manner.

Blain and Sasha were in their quarters exhausted sitting looking out at the cosmos thru their window when to their amazement they saw Emily outside. She was smiling and waving to them. They thought that perhaps they were hallucinating.

Emily floated thru the view port window and stood before them. She was radiant but looked physically the same.

Emily walked over to Blain and gave him a fierce, close, hug.

"Oh Blain, I missed you and Sasha so much!"

Emily then reached for Sasha and included her in a communal hug. Tears of joy and relief flowed all around. Emily infused their spirit with strength and peace. Indeed, they had not realized how weak they had become. Emily walked them over to the bed and both Blain and Sasha fell slowly to the bed in a deep and healing slumber. Emily thought sadly, they soon shall have peace. For whatever reason, the Great Cosmic Spirit wants them to receive their spiritual bodies now and no longer be corporeal beings.

While Blain and Sasha slumbered on the bed, Emily entered their mind and implanted upon their spirits the peace that passed all understanding and realize their work was done in the corporeal form. They would return to the earth but it would not be with the fleet of Carriers.

CHAPTER 38
IMMENENT ENEMY ARRIVAL

It had been a year since the beach attack. Sara had her command on alert with half the fleet on duty and the other half on recreation and relaxation with a ninety-day rotation. The individuals serving on space stations and various moon basis throughout the solar system served a six-month rotation. All the service members opted to keep their children on the Earth.

After the attack on the beach in which a large number of casualties was incurred, it was decided that information would slowly begin to be released to the general public so they could prepare a defense and not be caught unaware.

The President and the World Council was the first to get a briefing as to what actually happened on the beach. About half of the members believed what they were told was a fake scenario which was enacted by an elite inner circle which wanted to rule the world, the other half was dumfounded and truly did not know what to the think. And then when they found out about the Andrians who helped them defeat the alien entity, they really got hostile. It would not be polite to say what they thought when they were introduced to Muskula. Some believed

Muskula was a circus freak. And most were in fearful denial deluding themselves that what they heard was not true. Sara believed it to be wise and prudent not to say anything about sending young people into space or to reveal what Emily had said about, "The Point of No Time".

Sara was fairly sure that the reaction of the World Council was but a microcosm of what would happen when the rest of the world found out about the on-coming slaughter. Sara did not have the heart to tell them they were all doomed and the earth would be totally destroyed. She did not have the heart to reveal that the end of time was near.

Sara contacted Jawane and said, "Jawane, it is time to get the world religious leaders together again and tell them we have new information. Someone has to give the earths inhabitants hope."

It was not long before the sightings of saucers and drones became too numerous for the story of the Andrians to be contained from the general population. In fact, they were beginning to become hostile to the military and government for their continual denial. Charlene James just could not keep up with the sightings and writing cover stories. She called Sara and asked if they could meet for lunch somewhere on the Georgia cost.

Sara was pretty sure she knew what Charlene James wanted to discuss so she decided to bring Jawane along. She selected a private restaurant on the ocean front with a patio lined with flowers and sweet, smelling gardenia bushes. Sara felt like she needed a little nostalgia and the façade of normalcy to provide a short escape of the crushing demands of working to save as much of the population as possible, Human and Andrian.

It was amazing how the Andrian children flourished on the earth, many of them were actually laughing and smiling. All of them loved exploring the woods around the base property and some even learned to ride horseback.

This kind of time out for Sara was almost non-existent, thus her desire to share the time with Jawane. Sara was sure she was going to bring Commander Frank Morningstar. It appears they found a soul mate within one another. That too would soon pass, at least on the earth.

Sara arrived at the restaurant at nine in the morning just to sit on the patio and enjoy the view of the pristine waters. She did not waste her time on reverie altogether. It was a quiet time when she could do her best thinking and planning most all of which took place in her subconscious. Sara sipped on a mint julip with her eyes closed listening to the waves gently rush up onto the beach. In addition to the sensory perceptions of taste and sound, Sara could almost taste the heavenly fragrance of Gardenias and Magnolias. A long voyage without the beautiful treasures of Earth's fauna would be a sad voyage indeed. There was a veritable army of botanist and scientist insuring the Inter- Galactic Arks and Carriers were packed with most all of earths treasures.

Jawane sat silently beside Sara enjoying the moment. They wanted to have children but their demand for duty precluded such a luxury. However, Grandma Flata preserved eggs and sperm for later use. They understood but did not admit that it was in case they both died they would still have offspring.

Sara was surprised but pleased to see that instead of Commander Morningstar accompanying Charlene James, she had Kyla in tow. Kyla in truth was somewhat afraid of Sara even though they went to school together. Kyla believed Sara had such an overpowering presence about her. She did not miss anything and seemed to be aware of everything around her. She incorporated the feline stealth of a black panther and the coiled spring of a deadly rattler.

Sometimes, the smile on her face did not reach her eyes and in times like that she was her most threatening, and Kyla believed with all her heart, deadly. Then there was the antipathy of her threatening persona, the men and women in the military literally loved her and would die for her at a moment's notice. She did not know what Sara had done to engender such worship, as that is exactly what it was, but it was awe inspiring.

And, she and her children had been a benefactor of her allegiance and devotion to her friends and family. Her willingness to die for her was clearly demonstrated on the beach when the alien entity was preparing to kill her and her children and always brought tears to her eyes when she thought of the love Sara had demonstrated for them. And then, because of her selfless sacrifice for them, they were incorporated into the military milieu and became family that would receive all the rights, privileges, and benefits of one that is beloved by Sara.

Sara stood when Kyla and Charlene James approached. The women embraced and talked all at once kissing one another on the cheek.

Charlene James said, "Oh Sara, it has been too long. I feel like I have been left out in the cold and am being stretched in all directions at once. Actually, I feel like a chicken with my head cut off".

Jawane snorted as an image of Charlene James with feathers and no head running in a circle squawking, flapping her arms.

Sara rolled her eyes as she saw his thoughts and responded with, "I have been following your work and I am amazed how effective you are."

Then looking at Jawane she said, "Don't you think she is organized Jawane?"

Charlene James looked at Jawane and saw a face with a broad smile go to a solemn look as he responded, "I do Sara, she is very organized."

Charlene James thought for a second remembering what Kyla had said about him being a very strange duck.

Jawane's face broke into a smile again.

Sara continued, " I especially liked the way you deflected the comments by the small, town mayor in Arkansas. How dare he accuse the military of covering up the construction of moon bases on the dark side of the moon! Where did he get such an idea?" Everyone laughed.

"But seriously Sara, we have to do something. Why do we not bring the Andrians into the light? There have been so many leaks out of the World Government Council that their signed, sworn statements to secrecy, mean absolutely nothing."

"Jawane smiled and said, "Great, we can all do Emily's circle dance with horns telling them to take us to their leader".

Sara and Jawane laughed heartily as they, and all the children, had been taught the circle dance well by Emily and videos of Jawane and his Sister Hanlee interrupting the very first grand council between Humans and Andrians on the Andrians Intergalactic Carrier, when they were about age twelve, has been circulating for years. At that point in time the Andrians absolutely, without a doubt, had no sense of humor. On the Andrian side of the room there was absolute, steely, stone cold, silence. On the Human side of the room men and women literally howled with laughter until tears flowed throughout. Part of the release was the certainty due to the fact that the Humans were in the presence of a race of beings that could literally wipe them from the face of the earth, and some disgruntled members initiated a program to do just that.

Sara said, "I think you are right Charlene James and I believe that the sooner the better. However, Muskula and her people should remain in the dark along with the Neanderthals until the very end. Not much will matter what people think and believe then, they will be the least, scariest thing."

"Jawane and I have been talking about perhaps it is time to bring in all the world religious representatives and begin to release hints of what is coming. Most of them are aware of the Andrians presence and they know of a conflict being waged in a faraway galaxy against another alien entity but due to distance they believe it does not concern them. They have unilaterally decided not to enlighten their congregates of the Andrians because it does not seem to fit neatly into the orderly doctrines of their religion. Some leadership is being provided by different churches but fear of the unknown slows down enlightenment."

Sara responded, "Yea, everyone wants to go to heaven but no one wants to die to go there. And, it is so much easier to live the here and now and let the world of tomorrow take care of itself. I kind of like that idea myself but we all know our time is shorter than previously believed and people do have a right to know what is coming so they can make their peace with whatever creator they believe in."

Jawane looked out toward the water with distant, focus in his eyes then said, "The clergy's of the world need to begin mentoring their congregates in earnest and prepare them for the terror that is coming. And if the attack at the beach is any indicator of what is coming, then sheer terror is what it will be as there is no stopping them. Faith in a Supreme Being is the only thing I know of that will give anyone hope."

Everyone sat quietly with their thoughts. Sara looked at Jawane speculatively. She had never heard him voice his personal beliefs in a Supreme Being but after they were visited by Emily and she took Grand Ma Flata, they all had major shifts in their beliefs and understanding of what was to come. They were the lucky ones, enlightenment helps but it does not negate faith.

Kyla sat quietly listening to the discourse. Strange they were discussing the end of all life on earth as if they were at a nice Sunday tea with friends. She had not paid too much attention to whom else might be present on the patio but upon looking around she again noticed the large number of space intelligence commandoes guarding Sara and Jawane. There were no vacant tables for up to thirty feet. All of them were dressed casually and each wore a smock of one design or another which concealed the exotic weapons she knew they carried.

Kyla was caught unaware of the drift of the conversation and she was startled when Sara asked her what she thought of their plan. Sara smiled as she read Kyla's thoughts, she was actually eying one of the good looking Andrian Agents at a far table. Sara also noticed that the Agents Face turned red as he too could read her thoughts.

"Oh well, such is life", thought Sara.

"Kyla, we decided that it is best to set up a meeting with the major world religious leaders under the guise of a conference regarding teaching religion on long range space flights. We believe everyone would like to participate and no one will feel threatened."

"Charlene James, can you set this up within sixty days? I know it is quick but we can add an incentive for attendance by transporting them on military aircraft out of five major airports."

Jawane said, "Why not sail them around the moon to get their attention? We are going to tell them basically everything except the ending so why not show them the work we are all putting in to fix the problems. It will also open their eyes to help insure them that Andrians are not the enemy but an equal partner. However, I believe the seed carriers should remain a secret as much as possible. Things are going to get really nasty as it is."

Sara responded, "That is a good idea Jawane. I imagine after they see the other side of the moon with all the construction and manufacturing of space craft that the idea of God and long-range space travel will not be uppermost in their minds. They will take to heart the seriousness of our shared mutual dilemma."

CHAPTER 39
CHANGE OF FATE

Blain and Sasha awoke from their deep induced slumber and stretched slowly on the bed. Neither realized how exhausted they had been. They did not know how long they had slept. Having spent years on the battle front continually evading a sure death as they attempted to slow down the advance of the alien entity their minds never had a chance to achieve the deep rem sleep, balancing ones' perspective. They had already given the command that all Carriers should prepare to return to Earth and their Carrier was to be the last to leave.

The loud blaring of an alert sounded over the ships' intercom.

"Attention all personnel. Incoming enemy missiles!"

Blain and Sasha made their way to the bridge after donning their acid resistant battle armor. This was the first time the enemy had fired missiles at them. Evidently, they did not want the fleet to leave and was targeting their Carrier because they knew they were the command and control. Blain sent messages to all Carriers to depart immediately.

Standing on the bridge Blain and Sasha observed the advance of missiles coming ever closer to the Carrier.

"Captain, avoid missiles as much as possible but keep shifting quadrants now every three minutes. I think the missiles are supposed to be a distraction to enable them to board."

Blain had no sooner said the words when another alarm sounded indicating that a successful boarding had breached the engine room. Soon three more alarms sounded and also announced successful boarding's in three additional different locations.

The ship pitched wildly as the Captain reversed engines with thrusters firing in different directions in an effort to dislodge the spatial time warps the enemy aliens had successfully attached to the Carrier. Only one-time warp could be dislodged dumping the enemy aliens into space. The other three-time warps could not be dislodged.

Sasha caught Blains gaze. Words were not required between two seasoned warriors. They both knew their time had come.

Blain said, "Communications, send message to Carrier which is number two in Command and tell them they are now in control."

The crew battled the enemy which poured into the ship like mud. The dead piled up to the ceiling and began flowing down the sides of the heap with the living incoming alien entity's competing for space with the dead.

Blain placed an arm over Sasha's shoulder and keyed the ship inter-come.

"I would like to thank you for serving with me and trusting me all these years. It has been an honor to be your Commander. We are unable to dislodge the spatial time warps, therefore we know our fate is sealed. However, I propose to end this encounter in a somewhat different scenario than the one presented by our enemy. We are going to crash our carrier into their command ship and detonate our neutron generators at time of impact. God speed to you all.

"Captain, set course to enemy command ship and prepare for detonation."

Captain responded, "Yes Commander."

The response was stoic and calm just like accepting tea and saying thank you.

Blain took Sasha in his arms and kissed her gently on the lips.

"I never knew there could be such happiness in all the universe until I met you and Emily. I am not worried about dying. After all, you and Emily brought me back from the dead one time before, I am sure you can do it again."

"I love you Blain, I know this will not be the end but it is to be a new beginning. After all, Emily told us to go to the earth as quickly as possible and I suppose being a spirit being is the fastest. Evidently the fleet will not arrive in time."

The crew, knowing they were going to die in a neutron detonation, left the battlefield to the enemy confining them in locked and sealed compartments. They would eventually break out, just in time to be incinerated.

The Captain read out the time of impact and detonation over the ships' intercom. Everyone spent the time saying it was an honor to serve with one another. The enemy, caught by surprise by the suicide maneuver, attempted to move their cruiser away from the incoming carrier but to no avail.

Blain held Sasha in his arms and both had tears streaming down their face, not because they were scared of dying, but because they knew they would miss their children and would not see them again in this life. Blain held his hand over the self-detonation button as the Captain continued the count down. Blain kissed Sasha, his beautiful wife, one last time and pushed the button.

The Intergalactic Carriers leaving the space at the speed of light were quickly overtaken and bathed in neutrinos and other debris caused by the explosion of the two huge Inter Galactic Warships. The flash of light appeared to be a small supernova.

The Commander in the second in command Carrier advised in a monotone voice void of emotion, "Fleet, be advised I am now in command."

All sent messages responding an acknowledgement in the change of command.

CHAPTER 40
NIGHT TERROR

Pablo Salazar Esconera rode out of the corral on his large male stallion. The starry Argentine night was pristine with a slight chill and no wind. The full moon glistened like silver in the night sky. Pablo usually rode at night inspecting his small herd of cattle and riding the fence line looking for breaks. He preferred nights because that was when he could do his best thinking.

He enjoyed thinking about all the women he raped and murdered. He felt invincible and he really was. His father and brothers ran the small, town police department. The population of Caldera was only about thirty-five thousand. There was not a mother in his life as his father had killed her when he was five, he made his sons watch. He called her a whore and thus felt justified in his actions. That pretty much left the sons warped in their view of women. After all, the only women he killed were whores and of no value.

His neighbor's wife had slighted him and looked at him with hatred and disdain in her eyes. It was no secret in town among the women as to the manner of men he and his family were. They steered clear of them and warned their daughters to do the same. The department had only twenty officers and they took their own liberties with whomever they chose.

TARGET EARTH

A movement caught the corner of his eye. His stallion snorted, neighed, and reared up coming to a halt. Pablo saw four cows running full speed toward him. They appeared to be terrified with eyes wide and mouths frothing, and yet they ran into his horse knocking the horse down pinning his leg under the horse. Their fear was so great they never saw the horse and rider. His horse got up and ran away at full gallop following the terrified cows.

Pablo hobbled to his feet and could barely put his weight on his foot. Taking out his cell phone he called his father and told him what had happened and that he was stranded about a mile East of his house along the fence line.

Pablo saw something about five feet tall coming toward him. It had eyes all around its head and short tentacles coming out all over the body. There was no doubt that the creature was a demon coming to claim his soul for the evil he had done and was going to deliver him to the devil in the depths of hell.

Pablo screamed into the phone about the demon devil and he could not run away. Then to his father's astonishment he heard his son call out to God to forgive him for all the sins he had committed. A blood curdling scream was abruptly cut off as the phone went dead.

The senior Esconera immediately called his other two sons. "Pedro, get Michael and run over to Pablo's. He called babbling something about demons and the devil. Then he actually started praying to God to forgive him of his sins. His phone cut off in the middle of a blood curdling scream. He is on the fence line just east of his hacienda about mile. Take five officers with you."

"Yes sir, Papa", responded Pedro.

Pedro called the station on the police radio. "Dispatch, this is Pedro, send five police officers to my brother Pablo's farm about one-mile East of his hacienda. He should be somewhere along the fence line. He was babbling something about demons before his phone went dead. Michael and I are also enroute. Papa is coming too but he is on the other side of town."

Pedro and Michael rushed from their respective homes and met at their brother's hacienda. Together they drove the fence line East of the house. They saw several cows that appeared to have been stripped of flesh. There was not any blood. Michael stood up in the jeep thru the roof area and braced his 30-30 on the sill in front of him.

After turning on the spot light Michael spotted Pablos horse grazing near the fence line. Michael quickly moved the light away to look for Pablo. Then he returned to the horse because something did not look right.

"Pedro, go over to the horse next to the fence line, drive slow."

As they approached the horse both Michael and Pedro gasp. The bones of the whole horse was leaning against the fence and as with the cattle they had previously seen, it too was devoid of flesh and blood.

Pedro called his father on the cell phone and told him what they had found. "We will keep looking until we find him. Keep your radio on so I can contact you quickly if need be.

The five other officers arrived in their individual

squad cars and they too observed the horse remains. Three of them made the sign of the cross even though there was not a spiritual bone in their body.

Michael said, "We are looking for Pablo. Have your guns ready. He was screaming something about demons before his phone went dead."

All the officers exited their cars and fanned out on either side of the jeep which was in the lead. The sea of grass was only waist high. Pedro thought he saw movement about twenty yards ahead but he could not quiet discern what it was. The things he saw actually looked like tree stumps with short branches. Looking thru his binoculars he saw individual creatures with tentacles in front of an undulating mass of thousands of the creatures.

Pedro screamed, "Get into your cars and get out of here. There are thousands of demons here. Hurry get back to town!"

Due to the fear and trembling in Pedro's voice the officers did not have to be told twice. They broke and started running the fifty yards to their cars, each man for himself. Pedro turned toward the fence line trying to turn around only to drive into a sea of undulating creatures that he had not previously seen. Pedro screamed in his mike there were thousands of demons everywhere then his microphone went silent.

Michael fired his rifle steadily killing a dozen or so alien entities but just as the military found out, he learned it was to no avail. He was inundated in acid and his body melted from its frame as his skin fell to the floor of the jeep leaving his skeleton draped over the roof of the jeep, rifle still in his bony hand.

The other five officers ran to their vehicles like demons were after them, and indeed there was. All of them made it to their cars and managed to speed away from the field heading back to town which was ten miles away. They each went to their homes and after collecting their families they headed North leaving the towns people, whom they were supposed to protect, at the mercy of the alien entities.

Selena, the police dispatcher, who had heard the cries of terror on the radio called the chief immediately and told him what had happened. None of the officers answered their radio when she enquired as to what happened. While standing looking out the front window of the small police station she saw the five cars speed by at a high rate of speed none of them stopping. They were the only officers on duty.

Selena grabbed her purse and left the station. After arriving home Selena collected her two children, threw food and clothes into a suitcase and she too, left town going North. She did call the chief and tell him what she heard and saw and told him she was leaving with her family. Her last words she heard from the chief was him calling her a whore and all kinds of names and screamed she was fired!

After Senior Esconera heard his son's report and then the screaming on the radio about demons, he left his girlfriend's house and started driving to the ranch. He had not gone far when he was ran off the road by the several police cars racing from the area at a high rate of speed.

TARGET EARTH

One car driving by slower stopped to see if he needed help. The officer told him both his sons were killed by the demons and they were moving toward the town. He told him there were thousands of them and they covered the land and after they passed, they left nothing alive, then he too sped away.

Senior Esconera called his closest friend, the Mayor, using his cell phone. "Javier, all three of my sons have been killed by the demons. I saw all the police cars leaving the area at a high rate of speed. One of them stopped and told me there were thousands of demons and they are headed to town. I am going to pick up my girlfriend and leave."

"I know about the men leaving. Selena called me and told me they had passed the station. She said she was going to leave too and try to get her children to safety. Good luck amigo and good bye. The mayor took his family and he too drove out of town.

About an hour later the alien entity fell upon the sleeping town and killed every man women and child there. That was the pattern repeated throughout the earth for the next two years.

The enemy picked safe, unprotected targets and was saving the most resistant for last.

CHAPTER 41
WAITING NO LONGER

The military received the warning of an imminent attack about four hours before the actual attack. The space station personnel observed multiple disturbances in the star field all around the earth. They knew that something was going to come thru and they were surprised it was not immediate like the enemy's previous entry.

The five Intergalactic Carriers guarding the solar system were unable to locate any type of incursion. They were standing by on full alert. The military on Jupiter was attempting to launch two seed carriers and they were busy escorting them to the launch area.

Then, without further warning, a large alien Intergalactic Warship blasted out of a wormhole at a high rate of speed followed by ten others. All of them bypassed Jupiter.

The early warning system was sounded. The military escorts for the two Inter Galactic seed ships instantly launched the Seed Carriers thru pre-programmed worm holes. They disappeared into the void of space. At least there was another one hundred thousand souls evacuated from the earth. They would in all probability be the last.

The five Inter Galactic war ships guarding the earth

launched neutron missiles at the ten alien war ships. Five of the ships were destroyed. The other six continued toward earth and began opening wormholes to off load the alien troops. Then on a different coordinate another large wormhole opened and ten more alien war ships entered the solar system and continued to earth. As if this was not enough twenty more warships came thru the other wormholes and they too off loaded their multitude of alien warriors.

The Andrian warships had their pick of targets as they began blasting away destroying ten more enemy vessels for a total of fifteen. They were able to succeed because the enemy was not interested in them, they wanted to get on the earth.

A total of forty-one enemy Inter Galactic war ships entered earth's solar system. A total of fifteen was destroyed leaving twenty-six enemy war ships which was busy off-loading a million troops per ship. And it would be naïve to believe there was only one inbound wave.

All the family received the alarm simultaneously as soon as there was an indication something was coming thru the star field. When each of them received the alert, they knew the dreaded day had come, earth was next.

Sara was personally responsible for getting Warren, Becky and Lilly to the relative safety of the main base at Emily's house. Sara silently landed the saucer on the lawn in the driveway close to Warren's truck. Several special forces members set up a perimeter around the house. Sara did not have time to change into civilian clothes and this was the first time Warren would have seen her in her battle uniform. Walking thru the front door without invitation Sara went immediately to the kitchen.

Warren looked up with alarm on his face then recognizing that the woman in the strange uniform was Sara, his face changed from surprised fear to a scowl. Becky was unaware of the alarm and upon seeing Sara she nearly fainted and grasped the back of a kitchen chair as she set down the coffee pot.

Becky said, "Sara how nice to see you today. I forgot you were coming by."

Then addressing Warren, she said, "I am sorry honey, I forgot to mention Sara was coming by this morning." She did not know what else to say and had no idea how to explain Sara's uniform.

Sara walked over to Warren and said, "Be at peace Warren, all is well."

Sara could see that Warren was resisting the insertion to be at peace. He was almost successful when Sara stepped forward and placed a patch on Warren's neck. He immediately was immobilized and went into a deep trance. Two men in similar uniforms entered the room and placed a levitating device beneath Warren's arms and strapped it across his chest. The device lifted Warren off his chair in an upright position and carried him outside and into the saucer.

Sara looked at Lilly and saw the tears in her eyes. "Your Father is going to be fine Lilly. He has a very strong mind and that was the only way we could get him to come with us to the safety of Emily's house. We are all going there now."

TARGET EARTH

Sara took Lilly's hand and they walked outside and up the ramp to the saucer. It had been decided to deposit them on Emily's lawn, if time permitted. Warren was taken to a secure padded conference room with unbreakable glass that overlooked the hanger area. From there one could see the multiple spacecraft docked in the area.

Sara hoped the view would bring some semblance of sanity to Warrens thought processes. It did not, he just became angrier. Warren knew he was irrational but he did not know why. Sara remembered what Emily had said about putting Warren in stasis until they were away from the earth during the evacuation. She did not want to do that.

She remembered how she felt when Emily had kept her in stasis. She was thirteen when she went into decontamination and then kept in stasis for three years and was not brought out until she was sixteen. She missed all her adolescent years. Her adjustment from child to adult in one night was difficult. In truth it took a lot longer and she was almost spaced. Were it not for Emily's imploring intervention, Blain would have spaced her in a heartbeat and without regrets; life on an Intergalactic Carrier was harsh by human standards. Sara did not want Warren to miss out on Lilly's childhood, nor did she want Becky to live in limbo basically like a widow, especially during this very trying time.

Sara had her security detail go to the house and fetch Becky. Becky had no idea about the secret base in the mountain and was surprised and apprehensive as she stepped into the elevator concealed behind a false wall in the kitchen. Stepping out into the bright lit tunnel that had now been squared, paved and lined with stone giving the tunnel more of a mall appearance. The mall appearance went away as Becky then saw the huge steel doors spaced at intervals going down the length of the passageway.

Stepping up on the gravity lift with her escort of four agents of Sara's security team, Becky began to fear for the first time for what she was about to see and learn. She was aware of Warren Jr's role in helping to select candidates for possible evacuation of the earth should it become necessary. But surly it will not become necessary.

As the lift exited the tunnel Becky caught her breath at the scale of the hanger which was literally filled from wall to wall with space craft of all sizes and descriptions. Drones move in orderly rows, some carrying loads on pallets and some sprouting all kinds of antennas in every direction. She also saw armed men and women at interval in positions overlooking the floor.

Sara met Becky and gave her a hug. "How do you like my office? We do not have any time to chat so lets' get to crux of the matter. I do not want to put Warren in stasis as Emily advised I should do, until we launch into space and then only if truly necessary. Should I do that I would leave you as a widow and Lilly without a father. Furthermore, we can use his magnificent brain if we can bring him out of his psychosis. Should we put him under there is no exact moment in time that we may bring him out again. It will all depend on wartime circumstances. I myself was put in decontamination for one month when I was thirteen but woke up three years later at age sixteen. I do not want that to happen to Warren."

Becky was flabbergasted. She had no idea that Sara even went to space at such a young age, or even why, much less having experience the trauma of losing some of the most definitive maturity growth years in one's lifetime. Then Becky felt a tinge of fear grow in her mind. Sara had said that she did not want Warren in stasis until we launch into space, not if, but when. Unbidden tears rolled down Becky's cheeks.

Sara could read Becky's mind and she locked her arm in her arm and walked her in a sisterly fashion into the building and up a flight of stairs. Becky saw Warren still restrained in the anti-gravity lift harness in a position so he could have a view outside the window and clearly see all the space craft lined up as far as the eye could see.

When Warren saw Becky, his face turned beet red if it were possible to turn any redder due to his pent-up anger.

"Did you have anything to do with me being restrained and brought here Becky!"

Before Becky could answer Sara said, "Warren I did. It is for your protection. I am going to try one last thing in an effort to try and help restore a little sanity and peace to your mind."

As Sara said that a door opened in the back of the room and an alien entity, also hanging in an anti-gravity restraint but behind a shield, was brought into the room by two special forces members.

The alien focused several of it's eyes on Warren who

was also similarly restrained as "it" was. They were only four feet apart. Warren was startled when the alien shot streams of acid from six different locations on it's body in an effort to kill him. The clear enclosure that contained the alien also contained the acid and mist.

"Warren, as you can see, the Andrians are not the only life form in our universe. This thing here is the only life form that is going to destroy all carbon-based life in our universe. That means you, Becky, Lilly, Warren Jr. and the rest of us. They have already destroyed an untold number of worlds without end."

Warren stared in horror. The shock to his system was total and complete. Warren threw up, emptied his bowels and passed out.

Sara said, "Okay guys, return the alien to the holding area and terminate "it" along with all the rest of them. Soon there will be plenty more where they came from."

Sara called for medics to retrieve Warren and clean him up.

"Becky, I wanted you here so you might help Warren thru this…crises, and also enlighten you as to what is coming. In all probability an innumerable host of these things will begin arriving soon. I think that you and your family should be safe here for the time being. We will fight them as long as we can. After that we will evacuate our people, those of us that are still alive, from the earth. We are following the direct orders from Emily."

"Becky, you can wait in the infirmary until Warren wakes up and hopefully, he will be sane when he awakes. I do not know when I will see you again. We are all going to be rather busy. Just help and take care of the children, they are our most precious commodity. There will be no more hiding the enemy from the public. And Becky, take special care of my brothers Warren Jr., Orion, and Perilain." Sara looked Becky in the eye to insure, that she got the message. Chills went down Becky' spine. With that Sara turned and exited the door that they had entered.

CHAPTER 42
FIRST ENGAGEMENT

Commander Morningstar had his headquarters set up in the Colorado Rockies. The mountains provided the high ground that Commander Sara said was necessary to successfully defend against the alien entity enemies and is to be used for their last stand before evacuation. In the two years since being made commander of civilian forces, he had traveled all over the world setting up defense zones with civilian groups that wanted to join the cause. He insured they had weapons and intelligence to make them as effective as they could be. They all knew the score and were aware none of them would survive.

The alarm sounded when he was briefing his command staff of the efforts the Andrians and Space commandoes were making to set up quick response units anywhere in the country that the enemy should land. The civilian commandoes were assigned to more sparsely populated areas consisting of small towns and a few cities.

The alarm indicated that a wormhole had been opened and their landing site was outside of Laughlin, Nevada. The only defenses there was a small border patrol presence. The area was designated as his responsibility.

Commander Morningstar initiated the response code into his communicator and twelve thousand men stationed in various locations around the country were mobilized and were transported to Laughlin within twenty minutes using the saucers provided by the Andrians. . It would not take long to get to their destination traveling in saucers designed to carry up to a five hundred men. Commander Morningstar traveled in his own saucer with his command staff of seventy men and women.

Upon arrival just North of Laughlin, Commander Morningstar observed a sea of undulating mass moving in one accord toward the small community of Laughlin consisting of a population of less than ten-thousand people. The Border Patrols responsibility in Laughlin was to warn and evacuate as many citizens as possible. Commander Morningstar did not understand why the enemy chose such a small population center to begin their attack, especially since there was over two million people just North of their location in the Greater Las Vegas area.

The saucers landed between the oncoming ever growing mass of the enemy and Laughlin, positioning themselves along a twenty-mile battle line. Their objective was to kill as many as they could and to hold them off as long as possible to evacuate as many people as they could. Considering the limited hi-way system it was not going to be easy.

Commander Morningstar landed his saucer in the middle of the line and upon taking up a position he was surprised to find Commander Sara by his side. The title was not protocol but all the Commandoes in the entire Intergalactic Fleet called her that, and she liked it.

"Commander Sara, why am I not surprised to find

you here?"

"Why Commander Morningstar, do you think I would want to miss the welcome party for our visitors! This is your area and your command but may I suggest that perhaps three tactical nukes at their entry point as a welcoming gift."

"Excellent choice Commander."

Commander Morningstar spoke into his command communicator, "Okay Captain Gerald, drop three tactical nukes at the entry point."

"Yes sir, Commander".

Within minutes three tactical nuclear warheads exploded in and around the entry point. The aliens that were in transit were exiting into a flaming hell, those on the ground within a five-mile area was vaporized.

The first shot of the Resistance had been fired. Both Commanders believed that it was a good beginning. At least it let the enemy know they were not running away and they were not fighting with spears.

"Commander Morningstar, do you know if the locals have been notified to evacuate with all haste", inquired Sara.

Before Commander Morningstar could answer a voice in his communicator reported that about one-hundred cars and trucks was exiting the city in route to their location. All citizens were informed of the pending invasion and each community that was not part of Commander Morningstar's' command formed their own militias. Evidently the group was part of their own militia coming to join the fray.

Sara said, "Well more the merrier. But they must be informed that we cannot defeat them here. Our objective here is to give the townspeople time to evacuate. Truly, that is what they should be doing."

Commander Morningstar replied, "Yea, I know you are right. But they are somewhat conservative and they are coming here to kick some ass. I am sure they will leave when we do. We will fight them all the way back to town then we too will evacuate and take up another position. This cannot possibly be their only attack point."

That idea had been weighing heavily on Sara's mind all the way here from the home base. She did not understand why they did not head to the large population centers.

The towns militia arrived and parked behind the saucers. All of them gawked at the saucers and the men and women in strange uniforms carrying even stranger weapons. They were startled when the tactical nukes went off.

Commander Morningstar said, "Captain Smith, tell them they are welcome to join us but make sure they know this is a holding tactic until the town gets evacuated and then we will move to new positions."

"And, tell them not to take any chances and get killed on the first day." Commander Sara said without smiling.

Everyone took up positions behind whatever cover they could and waited. They did not have to wait long. The undulating wave of the entity from the different dimension seem to float over the ground. They sprayed acid as they advanced. Every plant in their path dissolved. There was a large number of desert rats, rabbits and other small creatures fleeing in front of the hoard.

Commander Morningstar gave the order to fire at will. Laser weapons cut the beings in half. As the beings in the front fell the undulating wave behind them continued to advance. The town's militia were all armed with hunting rifles and automatic weapons and they could not fire fast enough to make a difference in the mass advancement of the alien beings from hell.

It was not long before a wall of dead beings more than ten feet high and just as much thick, began to stack up. The aliens could not get close enough to spray the defenders with their acid, however, as the defenders continued to fire the acid mist began to waft perilously close to them. Fortunately, the wind was to the back of the defenders and therefore offered some advantage.

Commander Morningstar said, "Retreat one hundred yards and form up again."

Sara responded by saying, "Intelligence advised that forty alien Intergalactic Warships entered our solar system. We were able to destroy fifteen of them, leaving twenty-six to offload their troops. We are getting reports that twenty-six incursions have happened all over the world and all of them are in rural areas like this one.

Commander Morningstar said, "They are testing our responses and do not care how many of them are lost. The ten-foot pile of alien enemy in front of us is a testament to that. They just climb over their dead."

Sara grabbed the militia leader standing next to her by the arm and said, "Captain Smith, we are not going to be able to defeat them here. Nor will we be able to keep them from overrunning your town. Take your troops back to town and help evacuate. Anyone or any living thing left behind will be killed."

The militia leader looked Sara in the eye. "Where did these things come from and how long have you known about them? Are you an alien too? I know we were warned about an impending disaster but the magnitude of this thing just was not part of the scenario and is not plausible."

Sara took the time to respond as she could read his mind. He was scared, angry, and sad as he read the writing on the wall, so to speak.

"Your right, we cannot defeat them but we must try. They have destroyed an untold number of worlds. They have boarded and killed three crews of five thousand men and women on three Intergalactic Warships. And no, I was born here. However, there are three species not of this world helping us to defend the earth. The Andrians are the predominant humanoid specie. They were intergalactic explorers when we were still in the trees. As of this time, they, and we, are the only species that has ever stood against them. That is why we are first on their agenda and their cost in casualties is of no concern. Now please, take your militia and evacuate quickly. Stay out of low valleys and caves. Keep to the high ground only, no exceptions." With that, Sara ran to her command saucer along with her contingent of space intelligence commandoes. The saucer landed one hundred yards away and again the commandoes lined up. The militia returned to their vehicles and sped away toward Laughlin.

Commander Morningstar and his militia, assisted by Commander Sara and the space commandoes, engaged the enemy ten more times moving back one hundred yards at each increment. At the end of the day the small town was overran by the enemy. Everyone was exhausted so Sara called in the regular army and had them take over to give all the fighters a chance to recuperate. Sara had the troops to move back one hundred miles to eat, rest, sleep and hopefully keep the faith.

"Commander Morningstar, we need to return to our respective commands and conduct an intelligence briefing on other parts of the country and the world. Place your second in command in control and have them continue the one hundred-yard incremental stands; it seems to work pretty well as long as the enemy does not change its tactics. I will do the same. I will make sure you have adequate reinforcements to give extra relief. And most importantly, do not become complacent as we know the enemy is just testing our defenses. They may well do an end run with extra speed to trap us."

"Yes Mam, I understand."

Commander Morningstar briefed his command staff as did Sara, then they boarded their respective saucers and returned to the command centers.

CHAPTER 43
LAST CLASS

Hanlee was excited the way her students was engaged in the discussion that proposed how terra forming a planet using moons and asteroids would be of benefit to a space traveling society. Some of their proposals were way out but that that kind of thinking is what would help them survive in a stressful environment. As she paced across the stage, she was enthralled as she could literally see her students taking the lesson to heart.

As for the students, they have never seen Hanlee so intense and focused in their lesson plans. She was brutal in her critique of what alternative actions should have been foremost in their mind when solving a particularly difficult hypothesis. There was no doubt in any of their minds that she cared about what they thought. Every day she proposed a new puzzle in three-dimensional mathematics which at the beginning of the semester was impossible to understand but now six months into the nine-month semester did not seem so foreign.

Hanlee stopped her pacing and turned to face her students. She had a look of anguish on her face and tears flowed unbidden down her cheeks. She did not say anything and appeared to be in a trance. The students were alarmed because of her uncharacteristic actions. She was always one of the most, happiest instructors on the faculty staff, and could make a dark day seem bright. However, all the students looking at her now were feeling apprehensive as to what had happened to cause her to be so obviously distressed.

Hanlee had listened to the alert that had been broadcast by Space Intelligence and knew they were out of time. She loved these young people and they deserved a fate other than what appeared to be waiting for them. Hanlee quickly composed herself, licking her lips and wiping her nose on her sleeve. She was thinking, "Wow! Have I become assimilated or what?"

"As you know, my name is Hanlee. What you do not know about me is that I was born and raised, until age twelve, on an Inter Galactic Carrier. My parents are currently on an Inter Galactic War Ship fighting an alien enemy from a different dimension one galaxy away from our current position. We have been unable to defeat this enemy. They are not carbon based as we are."

"My responsibilities consist of identifying and assembling young people such as yourselves as candidates to "save" if you will, by placing you on Intergalactic Seed Carriers. These Seed Carriers are then launched into the cosmos. The purpose of this program is to save the Human, Andrian, and other species from extinction. As of this date, I have selected and enabled over five thousand students to be launched into space in an effort to save a remnant of our species. They were unaware of the program and did not know their fate as they were placed in hibernation and will remain so for one-hundred years. When they are awakened, assuming they have not been discovered and destroyed by our alien enemy, they will learn the truth...that truth being that the earth is destroyed, and every living thing on this planet no longer exist. To this date we have collectively gathered five million souls and have launched them into space."

"I am sure you are thinking how a person could be so heartless as to basically kidnap anyone and send them off into space in such a callous manner. Now you will find out. I would like a show of hands of those of you that would be willing to take such a journey knowing you will never see your loved ones again, and that the chance of survival depends entirely on your ingenuity?"

You could hear a pin drop in the large auditorium consisting of two hundred students. There were no nervous laughs, no questions and each of the students believed in their hearts that their friendly teach was speaking the truth. No one raised their hand. They did not appear to want to volunteer. They were terrified. They all hoped this was a game to see how they would react. That hope was dispelled when eight men and women in uniform came into view either side of Hanlee.

"Now you can understand how one needed to be callous to do such a thing. The objective is to save our species. I truly love each and every one of you. I want you to survive. You are the best chance we, as a species, have of achieving this objective."

As Hanlee continued speaking eight more men and women entered the room from the side doors, closed ranks around her and stood with her in their mist. They were dressed in a strange military uniform and carried an unknown kind of weapon which was clearly visible.

"A lot of time and effort has been expended by a lot of people trying to locate you and get you to this college. I have tried to expand your minds further for you to think of the possibilities of the colonization of another planet and evaluate each of you to ascertain whether or not you are not only mentally capable but spiritually in tune enough to be selected as a candidate. You have been given the mathematical tools to assist you in space travel. Have our enemy not arrived today you would have been placed on a seed carrier just before the end of the semester in two months."

One of the students slowly raised his hand. "What if I do not want to go? Do I have a choice?"

Hanlee responded, "Because of the arrival of our enemy, I am giving you a choice. The choice is simple, you either live out your lives on an Intergalactic Seed Carrier or you die here on the earth very soon. I will not coddle you. I will not coerce you. I will not expend precious time and resources on trying to convince you. You make your decision now. I have a transport saucer large enough to accommodate all of you should you choose to evacuate, to transfer you to a Seed Carrier. The Seed Carriers are in orbit around Jupiter. If you choose to leave only carry the small device, I gave you at the beginning of the semester."

"So you can make an informed decision it is important for you to know from what you are fleeing. This short video is from a distant planet that was destroyed by the alien entity from a different dimension. It was a water world occupied by an amphibious lifeform we call mermaids. A small remnant of their specie was saved by Emily Smith and several Space Intelligence Commandoes."

Hanlee had a holovision show the mass of the aliens as they came out of the water onto the ground. A large female with flaming red hair and male mermaid, bare from the waist up, along with about twenty more beings were firing rods with electrical discharges, into the mass. Suddenly a woman ran in front of them, kneeled down and fired a laser weapon that cut the enemy in half. Several commandoes took up positions either side of her and did the same. She motioned for the two mermaids and the rest of their specie to follow her up the ramp and into the saucer, which they did. A view of the saucer lifting off of the ground showed the aliens angrily jumping up and down at having their prey escape from their grasps.

"That was on a distant planet in another galaxy. Every living thing on the planet was destroyed except for those saved by Emily Smith. Now I want to show you an incursion closer to home. This happened two years ago on the East coast."

Hanlee showed a video of the same alien entity coming out of the water and being engaged by the military in strange uniforms, some in the air on floating platforms. They also saw Sara's heroic "save", of a woman, and of Sara being sprayed with acid and falling to the ground. She was quickly picked up by commandoes. The film did not censor any scenes and was not edited so it also showed people being dissolved to the bone.

"Our military was able to destroy them but there was

a large loss of life. The attack was covered up and reported as an accidental explosion of a chemical warfare agent aboard a naval vessel. The military also believed the attack was an intelligence gathering mission to test our response. Well, they are back in large force. We do not know how long we will be able to hold them off. They will destroy the earth and every living thing on it."

"You need to know in your hearts you are not abandoning your loved ones. You are assuring that their offspring and legacy survives. Now, no more words. If you want to leave on a Seed Ship, exit to the parking lot and literally run up the ramp and you will be assisted in assuming the proper position for takeoff. Those of you that do not want to go, please remain seated, and, may the Cosmic Spirit be merciful to you."

Hanlee walked off the stage with her armed guards and exited thru the side door to a separate saucer. All but five students chose to exit to the transport saucer to be taken to Jupiter.

CHAPTER 44
PAIN OF LOSS

Sara was in the command center when a radio transmission came in advising that the fleet had returned and in dire need of rearming. She was further advised there were one hundred and twenty Inter Galactic Warships.

"Commander Sara to incoming fleet, who is broadcasting this transmission?"

"I am Commander Shirly."

Commander Shirly was evidently Andrian and saw no further need to expound on her ascension to command.

Sara had an ice, cold stab of fear slice thru her heart. She knew before she even asked, "Commander Shirly, what of Commander Blain and Commander Sasha?"

Commander Shirly felt the question was unnecessary. The answer was implied with her being in Command. However, she was aware of the love humans had for Commander Blain and Commander Sasha so she measured her voice carefully. She knew that even some Andrians had become infected with the human emotion of love.

"Their intergalactic ship was breached by the enemy. There was no way the Captain could dislodge them. This was the third boarding. Since there was no way to keep the enemy from boarding the ship, Commander Blain gave Fleet Command to Captain Averiall. Commander

Blain then ordered the Captain of his vessel to crash into the enemy Carrier which he did. Commander Blain then blew both ships up with a neutron bomb."

Commander Averiall's ship was also boarded and he responded likewise after passing on Command to me. The enemy fleet is not too far behind."

Sara dropped to her knees screaming and crying asking why the great Cosmic Spirit would allow such a thing. Tears flowed unabated and in effect, she was temporarily unable to Command. Sara's second in command in the command center resumed communications with the fleet commander and using his staff arranged for the Inter Galactic warships to rearm by sending out a fleet of arms carriers to their location.

So great was Sara's pain that she passed out on the floor of the command center and had to be transported to the infirmary where Grandma Flata tended to her needs. Sara woke several hours later and was at peace. She knew where she was at but she did not know why she was there or how she come to be there.

Perilain and Orion came into the room.

Orion said, "Hello big sister. We are glad to know you are feeling better. You have been asleep for ten hours straight. Grand Ma Flata took good care of you."

"I do not know how you could sleep so long knowing that you were supposed to fix us dinner tonight. You are negligent in your household duties."

"We would starve it wasn't for Persha! She is really a good cook," said Perilain.

Sara looked at Orion and Perilain. "What happened?

Why am I here?"

Orion and Perilain looked at one another. They did not know what to say or rather what not to say.

Sara tried to read their minds and for some reason everything was fuzzy and muddled. Fortunately for the boys Grand Ma Flata came in and said, "Okay boys, you can leave now. You should be satisfied now that you talked to Sara and you can see for your selves she is okay."

Both boys gave Sara a hug and a kiss on the cheek, murmured that they loved her and turned and left the room.

Sara was surprised, she could not remember the last time they hugged and kissed her and told her that they loved her.

"What is going on Grand Ma Flata? What is up with them?"

"Well they insisted on seeing you. They wanted to see for themselves that you are okay."

Flata turned serious and all business. "Sara, you have been under tremendous stress as Commander of the worlds Space Intelligence Defense. You have engaged in two very extended combat scenarios with the alien entities. And you know that the end is near. It is only natural that you should feel compressed beyond measure upon hearing of the passing of Blain and Sasha."

Flata observed Sara closely. Sara had an aneurism and could have easily died had she not been brought immediately to the infirmary. The stress upon her was more than most humans could stand.

When Sara heard about Blains and Sasha's passing

again, she felt a dull ache in her head. Flata had placed a block on her emotions so as not to cause undue emotional stress. "Be at peace Sara, all is well."

Flata took hold of both of Sara's hands. "Child, I know we are going to miss them, we all are grieving. But it will only be for a little while. We both know that death is only a transitional state to a different sphere of existence. I know that because I have been there with Emily. I cannot begin to tell you of all the wonderful and marvelous things I have seen that the Great Cosmic Spirit has prepared for us. And soon, because our fleet has arrived, with our enemy not far behind, "The Point of No Time", is certainly upon us and then we will all transition to a different sphere of existence. Whither we will be translated or resurrected I do not know."

"We know we must do battle and in all probability some of us will be taken before "that time". Until then we are to send as many of those things as possible to their eternal damnation. I think you are well enough now to get up and take an exercise walk. There are a lot of concerned people who want to see you for themselves."

CHAPTER 45
PRELUDE TO FINAL ENGAGEMENT

The five Andrian Intergalactic Warships began picking off the twenty-six Alien warships. The aliens did not try to resist. They opened hundreds of worm holes to off load millions of their troops. As long as the Alien warships were not destroyed, they continued their one objective, offload their troops on the earth.

The mystery of why they only landed in sparsely populated areas was an advantage for earth defense forces as it gave them time to form chains of defense in open areas. The enemy was easily thwarted and slowed in their advancement to whatever objective they were trying to achieve. The sparsely populated centers were easily evacuated.

Muskula met Sara in the Foyer of the hospital and they hugged silently for several minutes. Both women had tears in their eyes.

Muskula said, "We have to talk Sara. The enemy is using totally different tactics here on earth than they did on our home world. They are stalling. There is no good reason for them to do that. They are obviously staying away from the major population centers. Perhaps that is the objective, to move the population into large groups to more easily kill them. The next tactical move could possibly be just spraying the atmosphere with their acid and not even landing."

Sara walked arm in arm with Muskula over to a large couch and they both sat silently looking at one another. Each woman knew what the other was thinking.

"When they attacked your home planet, did they go directly for the population centers?", Sara asked.

"They did. It was a surprise attack. More than half of our population was killed before the first sun cycle. It took them two more sun cycles before they destroyed us from the planet. We were done for but Emily showed up and saved the remnant of our species. I think they are just waiting for their fleet to arrive. It cannot be too much longer now. I imagine when they do arrive the extinction will not take two years but just a matter of days."

Sara sat thinking a minute. "I guess it is time to warn the World Council and The President. We obviously cannot think that we can keep the secret any longer. We should tell the population about everything. Of course, that does not include any information about the Seed Carriers or about the few of us that will escape. Even though we are called to perform a spiritual overwatch function I am sure they will not accept that and will think we are abandoning them. We will tell them about the extinction and about the potent. Many will not believe. But after the landing and destruction of Laughlin, most will get the message."

"I have talked to Charlene James and she already has a short loop projection of the fighting in Laughlin and the beach invasion ready for transmission. She said she will clearly denote whom she is and what her job duties have been in the past. She will start with the attack on the beach two years ago."

"Our five Intergalactic Carriers guarding the Earth have finally destroyed all of the initial enemy ships but not before they offloaded their troops all over the world. Their ships did not try to defend themselves. Their objective was obviously to drive everyone to the main population centers. I guess for the most part they succeeded in their objective."

Muskula said, "You know Sara, I do not believe that we will have a year or two years before the enemy arrives. I think it will be a matter of months, perhaps weeks even. And I also believe they will annihilate the world in a matter of days. Or at least try because we know they are bringing their whole fleet. We should make evacuation plans."

Sara rubbed her nose with her finger thinking. "I do not understand how "The Point of No Time", is to come about. Will it be before the attack?

Or, perhaps during the attack? Surly the Great Cosmic Spirit will not allow everyone on Earth to suffer such a painful, ignoble death. But then again, your world was destroyed along with an untold number of others. Why should the Earth be spared and receive a different treatment than was given to all the other souls? Maybe none of us are supposed to escape into the Cosmos although we have already launched over five million people to various destinations unknown."

"Well Sara, whatever it is supposed to be, and whatever comes about I believe we all have been doing what we are supposed to do. Remember, Emily said that our purpose is to lure the Alien Entity to the Earth. As much as they hate us that seems to be a very easy thing to do."

"It also means they have their free agency and can choose not to come so it is important that they do not get even an inkling that we are bait. Somehow and in some way, Earth is to become the jaws of the trap which for them there can be no escape."

Sara gave a short snort, "Ha! I never have before in my life considered myself to be some kind of bait."

"I think we should go to the house and have some tea or something. Let us enjoy a peaceful moment with our families. It could very well be our last one. And, I imagine Kalaleel misses you."

With that, both women exited the fortress hospital and went to Emily's house.

CHAPTER 46
A TIME TO WEEP, A TIME TO MOURN

"Thank you for giving me your vote of confidence thru the past few years. It is with a sad and humble heart I now give you to Captain Charlene James, Space Intelligence Communication Liaison Specialist."

With that, "The President", of the World Council, relinquished the podium.

Charlene James went to the podium and stood silently before the large assembly. The message she had to deliver was not one she envisioned in her fantasies and dreams all during her adult life. The news "scoop", of the lifetime, was not supposed to be the announcement of the end of the Human Race upon the Earth. However hard and ugly her words were going to be, everyone deserved to know the "truth".

"You probable are unaware of the conflict that has been ongoing in the cosmos in galaxies too distant to be concerned. However, the incident on the beach front two years ago should have piqued your interest. I covered the incident and told you that it was nothing more than a chemical accident abord a navy vessel in which all the sailors were killed and which also killed over a thousand beach goers. Yes, it was a tragic and sad accident, I said."

"Well, I lied to you. At the time it was necessary. The Space Intelligence Group which has been in control of information concerning all things space, deemed it necessary subterfuge. I lied to you about all the flying saucers, drones, mermaids and about everything else that has been reported that seemed not of this world. That was my job. Deceive you and keep the peace. However, the real truth is that it was an attack by an alien life form from a different dimension."

"Long before my time, a group of spacefarers came to the earth to see how we Humans have been taking care of our planet. They are from a distant galaxy and their home planet is called Andria. The Andrians have been an intergalactic police force trying to keep other intelligences in line and at bay from the planet Earth. Many have been assimilated on the Earth and walk among us. They, being highly intelligent, are teachers, scientist, and yes families. They serve in positions of leadership within our military and scientific community. But most importantly and too the salient point of survival, they are expending their very lives to save ours."

"There is a scourge and a menace coming to the Earth to destroy every living thing upon the planet. The encounter our combined militaries had with this alien lifeform two years ago is believed to have been a scouting party to test our defenses and gain intelligence."

"Now, we all know about the destruction of Laughlin and other small communities around the world. As of this time they have attacked only isolated communities. Their Intergalactic Carriers have been destroyed by the combined forces of Human and Andrian militaries therefore they cannot land any more forces. All the alien entities that have landed are either eliminated or is being eliminated as we speak. This is a war likes of which we have never seen."

"Which brings me to the main topic of our information section. We know there are a lot more of them coming. We have not had enough neutron bombs to generate black holes enough to receive them all. Everyone should go home and make peace with whatever deity you believe in. When they do arrive, we will continue to fight them until we are all dead. We also suggest a painless method to end your life in the final moments. They use a highly caustic acid that causes ones' skin to melt from the bones flowing like melted butter. It no doubt is extremely painful."

"When you are looking for defensive positions, stay out of caves, basements, valleys or any low-level place. That is their killing grounds. If possible, keep upwind and go to high elevations. You will not need to seek them out to attack them because they will seek you out to kill you.

"They fight in the open, in the water, and when they come, they come in waves like a carpet. It will not matter how many of them you kill; they just close ranks with more entities."

"Their appearance is absolutely the ugliest nightmare that you cannot imagine. Our primary objective is to take as many of them with us as we can. They will destroy the earth. On a bright note, perhaps the Cosmic Spirit will intervene."

The military has developed a liquid potent that when consumed, will immediately and painlessly put you to sleep. Suicide is not an acceptable way to end ones' life. On the other hand, neither is hanging around waiting for your flesh to be melted from your bones, or to be sliced in half by a jet stream of acid. If there is no way out, one should consider this as an opportunity to do so painlessly and mercifully. It is a much better way to go."

"Now, we are going to show the video scanner of the beach attack two years ago so you can make an informed decision and know in your heart this is not a conspiracy of any kind. We are of the opinion that if we are to go down, we will not go down without a fight. If these things, alien entities, have a collective memory, we want them to know that the only reason they succeeded was because of sheer numbers and not because of their skill. After the showing of the holo vid scanner this meeting will be concluded. You can pick up portents at the door when you exit. And, God speed."

Commander Morningstar and Charline James watched the group leave at the end of the program. The group consisted of all the worlds' religious and political leaders. Tears were flowing in hushed gasp; despair was heavy and the air was thick. Every ones' face was deeply creased with pain etched in sagging jowls with fearful, furtive glances too see if everyone was reacting the same as they.

Commander Frank Morningstar and Charlene James had become very close and even married in a church. Their love for one another was deep and intense as is normal for the binding of ones' heart during dangerous and unpredictable circumstances. Of course, the only thing predictable now was an assured death.

They never spoke of what they would do when the time came. Charlene James did know she would not leave her husband under any circumstances. And sadly, being the warrior, she knew that he would die fighting by his comrades. He would not take the free ride offered by Sara. Charlene James did not want to die but she also knew she would not leave her husbands' side. It took a lifetime to find him. They would die together, fighting their enemy to the bitter end.

However, unbeknownst to her, Commander Frank Morningstar had already arranged with Sara to have Charlene James transported to Emily's house at that moment when all was lost. He loved Charlene James with all his heart and he wanted to ensure that she and his child and thus progeny, lives on. Sara had told him that Charlene James was several weeks pregnant and she herself did not have that knowledge and was unaware of the pending development. The question now was, what would come first, the baby or the enemy?

CHAPTER 47
MIRACULOUS APPEARANCE

Muskula and Sara exited the house slamming the screen door behind them with a resounding whack. This practice had become a wholesome and comforting tradition with all the children. In fact, Sara already had a work order in place that the door frame and wooden screen would be removed prior to evacuation and put on their Intergalactic Carrier for safe storage.

All the children and their friends were present and waiting quietly and expectantly. Each had received the alarm and proceeded immediately to the house. It had been two weeks since the alarm but they were advised they could not leave the area thus they found things to occupy their time. Generally, they were entertained by Alice's guitar playing. She was really quite accomplished, and she had a voice with a wide vocal range that could hit high notes as easily as baritone notes.

A saucer landed on the lawn about fifty yards away. Several space intelligence commandoes exited the ramp with a woman in their mist. Upon getting closer they could see it was Charlene James. They were all surprised to see her without Commander Frank Morningstar as they had become connected at the hip so to speak.

They all stood as Charline James Morningstar approached. All the young people had seen holo vids of Charlene James fighting the alien creatures alongside of her husband Frank Morningstar. She had run toward them at one point and pulled a young boy from a wrecked car just before the car was bathed and dissolved in acid. She herself received serious injury and had to be carried from the scene. Her heroism had earned her the respect of all the militias.

She was no longer able to cover up the alien enemy. They definitely exploded onto the scene. Everyone was perplexed why they were staying away from the population centers. That was a good thing because it gave all the militaries around the world and the survivalist groups time to test their readiness. They proved to be very effective in holding and eliminating the scourge. There was so many of the enemy and many soldiers died gruesome deaths. Of course, they all were unaware of the approaching storm that was soon coming to the earth. At least the confrontations gave them bravado and a false sense of hope. That is the very least men doomed to death should have.

Sara approached Charlene James and gave her a big hug.

"It is so good to see you here. Thank you for coming. We have a lot to discuss. You need to stay out of the battlefield and start preparing our friends for what is coming. You need to impress upon them that they must choose only the high ground. You have to pound it into their heads that it cannot be anywhere else. It must needs be that they are engaged with the enemy as long as possible for, "The Point of No Time", to come about."

"Sara, do you not think that we should tell them all about the, "Point of No Time"?

"Are you speaking of the militias or the general public? We definitely are not going to tell the public, including the clergy, about that concept. They have no need to know. Now those standing on the wall, so to speak, who are dying daily, I think it only right we tell them. Space Intelligence knows this and they understand the commitment to die if necessary, to help bring about "the event". So yes, see that they are all informed. No doubt we only have weeks left."

As she said that she turned to her escort in charge and said, "Take Charlene to the Command Center. See to it that she is comfortable with refreshments and snacks and show her the communication system so she can send her information to all those standing on the wall, and then it will be time for her to rest."

Turning to Charlene James and smiling, Sara said," Charlene James, please accompany your escort to the Command Center and do your magic. I will be along shortly".

Hanlee was sitting nearby with Ricky and they were listening to the conversation. She had a heavy heart because she had been thinking of a young girl, thirteen years of age that was extremely intelligent. She had seen her on the video several months ago answering questions about the economy. It amazed her that she could interpret the graphics on economics. She was obviously a gifted child.

TARGET EARTH

Surly she did not deserve to die, but then who did?

Sara saw Hanlee's pensive look and read her mind regarding the child.

"Hanlee, go get the child and bring her here. But you must be quick. We do not know when the enemy will be arriving. I just feel like it is soon. Take at least one-hundred space intelligence commandoes and go in two saucers. You may have to fight your way home."

Hanlee looked at Ricky and said, "I want you to stay here. It is necessary for one of us to be available for our cousins. It has to be this way. Everything will be fine. I will return as soon as possible. If I do not see you here, I will see you on Jupiter. You cannot wait for me if you need to evacuate. Even if you do not see me on Jupiter, Sara will make sure we make it home and get us together."

Sara replied," Sounds like a good plan."

Jawane chimed in, "Sis, you want me to come with you"?

Hanlee walked over to Jawane and gave him a hug. "No thank you brother. It will be a short trip."

Ever since she was almost killed, she always hugged Jawane whenever she or he was going anywhere. Definitely not the Andrian way.

Just as Hanlee was about to leave, Emily Smith shimmered into view just about the ground.

"Hello family! It is so good to come to you in person." Laughing she added, "So to speak!"

"I am so proud of you for the work you are doing. The Seed Carriers will soon be translated to a new realm. A new day is dawning and just beyond the horizon. The destruction of our enemy is neigh. And most importantly, each and every one of you are safe."

Looking at Warren Jr. Emily said, "Son, I am so proud that you found your life mate! Did I not tell you that she played a mean guitar!"

Then looking at Alice, Emily smiled and came close and embraced her but only in a spiritual way as Emily did not have a corporeal body.

Alice could feel the embrace and the purity and love that Emily shared with her. Alice's heart was so imbued with untold joy and happiness she felt like she might shatter due to frailty of spirit.

"Oh Alice, my beautiful child. Allow me to share small minds with you."

When Emily said that, Alice seemed to turn inward and was immersed in two small developing minds. They were babies growing within her body but as of yet had no physical substance! How was that possible. The only thing that was there was their spiritual essence.

Alice gave a shout of joy and jumped into Warren Jr's arms. "We are going to have twins! It is a boy and a girl! Let's name them Adam and Eve!"

As Alice and Warren Jr. laughed and talked to one another, Emily turned to the group of young people, and Sara.

"I know you are sad because your mother and father are no longer present among you. But I assure you that you will see them again, and soon. The enemy is close by. And even now is preparing their invasion. You must prepare to leave at any moment. You each have done your jobs well and you should be proud as your efforts will show fruit upon the vine of plenty which grows into the eternities. Each of your names will be revered thru out the cosmos thru eons to come and within each and every dimension of the new order."

Then Emily looked at Hanlee. Smiling, Emily said, "Hanlee, nothing that we come across is by accident, everything happens for a reason, remember? The little girl in Seattle, Molly, she is very important and is to play a substantive role our future. Please, retrieve her quickly without delay. For her, we are all expendable."

Everyone gasped in amazement. What a statement of ones worth and value. And, by Emily no less!

Hanlee said, "Yes mam," turned and left the group and went inside the house and proceeded to her saucer. One hundred space commandoes accompanied her to Seattle.

After Hanlee left Emily spent one hour with the children imparting several messages, not only to them but the military also. She spent a lot of time on explaining every one's future missions and the role each would play.

CHAPTER 48
HANLEE'S MISSION

Hanlee had never been on a mission as a Space Intelligence Commando before. She was and always have been an educator, as was her brother Jawane. She was familiar with violence as she was assaulted on her very first camping trip alone and was nearly killed. But fortune smiled upon her and she was rescued by Ricky and his daughter Tiffany.

Hanlee may have been in charge of the mission but she had no illusions as who really was in control and that was fine by her. Her only objective was to retrieve the young girl, age thirteen. She was advised that due to the saucers size she would disembark one block away in a grocery store parking lot. Hopefully there would be room. The home was in an urban area with lots of residences.

There was no father in the picture as the mother was raped as a young teenager and impregnated by the rapist. The mother and daughter lived alone without any family support as she herself was an only child from a dysfunctional family. Neither parent believed their daughters story thus what little familial family bond that was present was breached beyond repair. She refused to get an abortion and was forced to leave home with the baby upon the baby's birth. Church charities was their mainstay but as usual, scrapping out a living as a very young mother on her own was more than difficult. There were times when she just felt like giving up but her daughter seemed to know just what to say.

It did not take very long for her daughter's intellectual abilities to become noted by academia and by the time she was ten they had a steady income due to her speaking at various universities and civil functions. Mom had no idea what she was talking about and was perplexed as to why her daughter was so smart. She just knew she had to protect her.

Both saucers landed in the almost vacant parking lot. The ramps dropped and the military contingent flowed out in an orderly manner going toward the end of the block on separate sides of the street with a few going down an alley which was back of the tenement building.

Molly heard a commotion of running feet and looked out her bedroom window to the street below. The whole area was filled with men and women in some kind of uniform of which was unrecognizable to her. All of them was carrying some kind of rifle with a flattened barrel.

"Strange gun," murmured Molly.

Molly saw a tall slender woman in uniform look up at her and smile. The woman disappeared thru the entryway out of view of her window. She had never seen her before.

"Mom! Mom! Come here and look at all the soldiers outside! Something strange is going on. I think they are here to arrest someone!"

Lori sauntered from the bathroom with her light linen

shifted pulled around her shoulders and tied loosely with a strap around her waist. Her black pixie hair, wet from the shower, was wrapped in a towel.

Looking out the window she observed the large contingent of military on the street. Some of them had turned away and had formed a line facing the intersection and had actually began firing their weapons which was lasers. She could hear screams from down the street and saw a small crowd of people running across the street intersection shouting. And then, to her horror she saw the same alien entities that she had seen on tv and the military was fighting in the desert and other remote areas, approaching the intersection.

The street looked like a gray flowing river convoluted in an up and down motion as the throng advanced. At about the same time the apartment door splintered and the tall blonde woman in the same uniform came in through the door.

"We do not have time to explain right now but you both are coming with us."

Having said that two of the soldiers strapped a device under their arms and lifted them off their feet and carried them out the door guiding them with their elbows. They were quickly rushed down stairs and outside. The firing was more intense. The screaming was louder and some of the cries were quickly cut off in mid scream. The group as one turned and ran up the street to the parking where the saucers were waiting.

The military had formed a ring around the saucers and were firing continuously in every direction. They ran

TARGET EARTH

up the ramp and the first saucer lifted off the ground and began firing a green laser that was flat and swept from side to side.

Hanlee ran up the ramp with Molly in tow. Once in the saucer she placed Molly within the tube and pushed a button. The tube closed and a device was inserted into Molly's mouth. Other commandoes did the same to Lori. Both women were terrified.

The saucers lifted from the ground and revealed that the aliens have begun their final destruction of earth and their targets now were the major population centers.

CHAPTER 49
EVACUATION

Hanlee had not been gone over one hour. Upon her return the mountain base was a beehive of activity. When they exited the craft there was shouting and clanging of alarms. The base was being abandoned. They were to all go to Jupiter. Hanlee had the two women moved to the Command Center.

Sara was in her element commanding different military units to stand and fight or to evacuate with all great haste. There was a large number of civilians that were being evacuated at the last minute as was Molly and her mother Lori.

Sara stopped and turned toward the two women as they took a seat in the corner still strapped to the levitating harnesses. They were hugging one another fearfully as they did not understand what had just happened and who these people were.

Sara walked over to the women and said, "So you are Molly. You have no idea how important you are and who told us to go and get you. Hanlee was going to do that anyway but was unaware of the gravity of the situation until Emily appeared and told her to go with all haste and not only that, but everyone was expendable but you. Wow, you must have a very important role to play in our future. Welcome aboard!"

Looking at Molly's mother, Sara said, "You must be Molly's Mom, Lori. I am Sara, it is an honor to meet you. You raised your daughter on your own and worked to give her every opportunity to help her succeed. I bet you were surprised to realize her intelligence level was way above everyone else in the neighborhood. Ha! I know that feeling, well not being the smartest. With the Andrians, I was way on the other end of the scale! Well, here she will be among her peers and she will finally get to talk with someone who actually can understand her! And in some cases, may be more advanced mathematically than she. Go ahead, stand up and look outside the window. This has been our Command Center since I was your daughters age. Of course, back then, the mountain had not been hollowed out."

"And, I would love to stand here with you and remanence and explain what is happening but we do not have the time. I will give you the short version. This world and everyone and everything on it will soon be destroyed. We are evacuating. Hanlee identified your daughter as a candidate to be rescued. Then our mentor and loved one appeared and said that it was imperative that your daughter be rescued and we ourselves are to be expendable in achieving this task. I do not know who your daughter is but evidently, she is vital to the future survival of the Human and Andrian species and others."

Lori was perplexed as to whom the "others", were.

All the young children came into the room and introduced themselves to Lori and her daughter Molly. Because of what Emily had said they were all very interested in her and were very intrigued as to what purpose she would serve in the future.

Sara said, "Ok family, we will take our last look in a low altitude flyover going to the West coast. You will never see the world so up close and personal again. Proceed to the transport carrier. We will fly to the Moon instead of Jupiter as that is where our Seed Carrier is waiting and where we will all board. We will stand some distance away and be witnesses to the destruction of the planet earth by the alien entity. In due time we will testify against them for the murders and deaths they have caused. Those were the instructions verbatim given to me by Emily."

With that said, Sara walked out of the office followed by what had become a very large contingent of family and friends. Lori and Molly followed behind being the last to be added to the group. They approached a large troupe carrier that held two hundred personnel. Upon entering the carrier Sara said, "Find a seat, filling the front to the back."

As Sara approached the front seating area, she observed Becky, Warren, and Lilly sitting together. Warren was heavily sedated and already incubated with the umbilical. Charlene James was sitting next to Lilly and she too was heavily sedated and incubated with her umbilical as well.

All the family took their respective seats without talking, each deep in reflection wondering if they should have or could have done something different or perhaps have worked harder to save more souls. They were pensive thoughts and weighed heavily upon their hearts. The thoughts were shared collectively and tears slid down their cheeks.

Sara, able to read the shared pain was equally silent as she too had the same guilt-ridden fears. How will future generations of survivors judge them for the way they chose whom to save and executed the evacuation plan?

Sara sat in the command chair and was enclosed with a membrane shroud which connected her to the biological artificial intelligent entity that resided within the saucer. The entity entered her consciousness and said, "Commander, your heart is heavy. You are to be commended for carrying out your duties as completely and efficiently as possible. No one could have done better. Blain, Sasha, and Emily, are proud of you and extend to you strength thru your coming trials."

Sara was perplexed, she thought their trials were basically over. They completed their assignment and were leaving the earth. What more could be required of her? Of them? The rest was just space travel. Or was it?

The saucer left the military base along with a thousand others. They left all accesses open in case some militias cared to make their last stand in the mountains. All the saucers went immediately to their designated Intergalactic Carriers, many of which was in the vicinity of the moon but most of which went to Jupiter. Those that proceeded to Jupiter were instructed to leave immediately upon arrival.

Sara flew just above the atmosphere and could see the thousands of wormholes that were opened from space to the earth as the enemy offloaded their millions upon millions of troops onto the population of the earth. The earth would be stripped of life within weeks, if not shorter time than that, perhaps days.

"Commander Sara. There are three life forms fleeing the alien entities three hundred miles ahead on an open plain. Everything else is dead within a thousand miles."

" Put the life forms up so I can see them."

Sara saw what appeared to be two riders on one horse. Moments later Sara was able to make out a male and a female on the horse. The female had long black hair blowing behind her head as they galloped full speed toward a precipice. She was also firing a rifle toward the side where Sara observed an undulating sea of the alien entity. Sara put the view using a holo-vid so everyone could see what was happening.

Sara asked her AI, "Do we have any seats available on our transport?"

The AI replied, "Yes Commander, there are two seats available."

"Prepare to land. I want ten commandoes ready to exit craft and secure a small island of safety for me while I get the two horseback riders."

As the horse approached the precipice it skidded to a stop rearing up on its hind legs throwing both riders to the ground. They knew they were dead, their only decision was on what manner of death they would choose, death by the alien beings acid melting their flesh from their bones, or jumping the eight hundred feet or so to the rocks below the precipice. They grasp each other in a lover embrace and shared one last, long, kiss.

The seventeen-year-old young man said, "Thank you for sharing our last days on the earth together Shana. Our love may have been short on the earth but we will be together thru the eternities in the Spirit World."

The young woman, fifteen years of age, looked up into his eyes and said, "Oh my warrior, the pain will only be for a moment. And you have been such a brave warrior. Our ancestors would have been proud of you."

They then heard the sound of running feet and as they turned, they saw a large airship of some type and about ten to fifteen soldiers in strange uniforms and caring strange weapons taking up positions around them and the airship. They began firing immediately using laser weapons which cut large swaths in the alien entities line slowing them down but not stopping the advance.

A young woman in uniform walked up to their horse and placed her hands on each side of his head. The horse immediately calmed and snorted a few times. The horse then walked to the young couple and placed his big head on their shoulders blowing warm air onto their necks. It was a form of communication they shared with the horse ever day since he was born and in the evening hours before they placed him in his stall.

Sara then placed a small light device on the temple and the horse went down on its knees, rolled over on its side and went to sleep and almost immediately quit breathing.

Turning to the young people Sara said, "Your horse is now at peace in the spirit world. His death was painless and quick. If you want to live then come with us. As you already know the earth is being destroyed and will soon be void of all life. There is no more time."

The young couple did not have to be invited twice. Hand in hand they ran to the transport followed closely behind by Sara. All the Space Commandoes followed suit. When the young people came aboard, everyone cheered and clapped. Saving souls was sparce and each and every one was precious and welcome.

The transport secured the access door and after everyone was seated, Sara quickly left the surface abandoning the earth to the alien entity from the Eighth Dimension. The trip to the Intergalactic Carrier was quick and no sooner had the transport docked than the ship left the area going beyond the solar system in less than a minute. As they were leaving, they passed an innumerable number of inbound alien warships going to earth. Neither was interested in the other. Since now all supplies was finite, nothing was expendable, especially munitions.

All the cousins born on the earth, which was basically all of them, were excited to at last be on the path to their destinies. The others picked up along the way were awed to silence and were fearful of what the future held. They reminded themselves and others that at least they had a future.

CHAPTER 50
A PRIVILEGE TO SERVE

The number of men and women on the plateau of the mountain was just a minuscule of those that were originally part of the force. The millions of military and civilian resistance fighters was now represented by a mere three hundred or so fighters still alive after the initial landing of the alien beings that was estimated to be in the billions. It was amazing that the military forces of earth were able to hold out for the three days when considering such odds. It was also estimated that over half of the alien enemy was destroyed.

The three commanders, Taaker, Sears, and Morningstar, stood in a circle around a pedestal that had a large red button on the top surface. They looked haggard, faces lined with grief and pain but their eyes! Their eyes were literally aflame with a fire of defiance that can be found only in the undefeated.

Commander Taaker looking down into the acid mist valley below said, "I would have never considered in my wildest of dreams that I would end my life's mission upon a planet."

Laughingly he added with pride, "Now Commanders Sasha and Blain, they knew how to exit from one's corporeal existence! I have cried many a night thinking of them and the joy they have brought into my life. They have set a warrior's path as an example how to die before one's enemy. And, it is not without honor. You know for an Andrian to shed tears under any circumstance is unheard of and unprecedented."

Turning to face the two men, Commander Taaker saluted and said, "It has been such a humbling honor to serve with both of you."

The two men returned the salute and acknowledged their gratefulness for his and other Andrians for their service to their home world, earth.

Commander Morningside said, "It is time gentlemen to say good bye to our friends and comrades in arms."

"Ladies and gentleman, it is thirty seconds before time to push the button. Therefore, it is time for us to leave so say your good byes. Thank you for your dedication and commitment. It has been a privilege to serve with you. And, God speed.

With that being said, the three men placed their hands over the large red button.

The enemy thought that the carbon-based lifeform which had killed so many of their kind, had given up. Therefore, they quicky began to ascend the mountain exulting in their long hard, fought victory. The end was finally here!

As the alien life form, came over the edge of the escarpment onto the plateau, the three men lowered their hands onto the red button and their corporeal form no longer existed. There was neutron, helium explosions half way across the continent as numerous bombs strategically placed, went off simultaneously. The explosion leveled not only the mountain they were on but also the surrounding chain of Colorado mountains.

CHAPTER 51
WITNESS

The central area of the Intergalactic Seed Ship had been modified so there was a large vacant area completely open to the outer hull. The open space was covered completely by greenery to be used for oxygen generation and water purification. The new growth greenery covered and area of a hundred miles long and fifty miles wide. The ceiling was covered with mist and clouds and was ten miles high. A thin double shield contained water circulation for cooling and protection from debilitating rays from the suns and cosmos and the hull was completely enclosed.

Most of the crew and all the passengers was summoned to this area to view the final destruction of the earth and hopefully, observe the beginning of, "The Point of No Time". A hola-vid of the earth and moon was in one area and of the solar system and cosmos in another.

Sara said, "Show me where my father is."

The projection of small point of green appeared in the middle of the continent. Upon magnification three men were standing off to the side of a small group of resistance fighters which was firing down upon the enemy alien.

Sara observed the three men salute one another and place their hands over a red button. Moments later there was a light flash brighter than the sun. The light explosion covered a third of the continent.

Sara saw the extinction of her father, Commander Sears ,and Commander Taaker, also a father figure, and Commander Morningstar. Unremittent tears rolled down her face as it did on all the people of the Intergalactic Carrier. They were truly the last living beings upon the face of the entire earth.

The magnification was reduced so the earth could be plainly seen just as if they were between the earth and moon. In the area of the cosmos view it appeared as if the stars were shaking and rolling and soon the view was a roiling mass of fire. The roiling mass began to pick up speed and soon became a horizontal elongated tube of stars and gas. There appeared to be nothing behind the mass as it was completely absent of light.

Looking toward the solar system and the earth, one could see a brilliant curtain of sheer light. The curtain was moving thru the solar system and it appeared to be corrugated with no definitive line transitioning from a solid to a gas. The front side was brilliant white and in the shadow of the corrugation it was the blackest black one had ever seen. As the wall of light move toward the moon an innumerable quantity of white sparks flew from the surface of the moon into the light. Also rising from the surface of the moon was red flashes of light which flew to the dark side of the corrugated curtain disappearing into the darkness.

As the curtain moved closer to the moon the surface began to shimmer and break apart and then flew into the curtain of light until the whole moon was gone.

The curtain steadily moved closer to the earth. The earth began to release a shower of light as the sparks flew into the light in a never-ending stream. After the last silver spark left the earth then a stream of red sparks more numerous than the white sparks appeared to flee the earth and moved into the corrugated dark side.

There was a momentarily and eerily quiet moment when nothing appeared to be happening. Then, extending from the dark side of the corrugated curtain, an innumerable number of long black fingers of tornadic spirals extended to the surface of the earth and acting as a vacuum, sucked all the alien entities from the surface of the earth. They too disappeared into the dark side of the curtain.

Of course, the earth was no longer habitable. All the water was grey acidic sludge. There was not a single green blade of grass left on the planet. But just as the moon disintegrated into the composite of molecular structures from which it was made, so too the earth began to break apart and its molecules began to be drawn into the light and it too soon disappeared.

Everyone in the observatory was crying and was suffering a great, deep, sorrow as they all saw the total destruction of the peoples of the earth by the alien entity. This is what they were called to do, to be witnesses. Then they heard a shout.

Everyone looked up and they saw the enemy fleet trying to flee the vicinity of the earth. Again, the spiraling black fingers reached out from the dark side of the curtain and sucked the alien fleet into the black abyss. It happened lightning fast. Not a single enemy ship or entity escaped.

Immediately after the enemy had been eliminated, the Intergalactic Seed Carrier holding fifty thousand souls began to vibrate. Sara and the children and the recent refugees grasp on to one another in a large group hug. Everyone thought they were going to die. There was a brilliant flash of light and immediately everyone was unconscious.

CHAPTER 52
NEW DAWN, DAY ONE

Flata awoke from whatever induced her to lose consciousness. She found herself laying on a matt of sweet smelling, green grass. She was still in the large cylindrical area consisting of the oxygen generating plants. However, to her surprise the whole area looked like a jungle. The small seedlings that were originally three feet high were now great trees. She could hear the sounds of many birds whistling and singing.

Looking up she could only see thin gray clouds and there was a gentle mist settling up on the foliage. She then noticed the smell of flowers and other sweet, smelling plants. Foremost and prevalent was the succulent scent of the Perilain flower, the same sweet smelling plant for which Sasha and Blain named their son.

Flata saw Sara a few feet away crawling to her knees preparing to stand up. Everyone was regaining consciousness and all were amazed to see the growth of the fauna.

Perilain was the first to speak. "That sweet odor is the Perilain flower. My Mom and Dad named me after the Perilain flower. I wonder if they came here while we were out and planted them. And these trees, they are slow growing. They must be at least more than five hundred years old!"

"Ok, listen up. Check and see if everyone is accounted for. I do not expect to find anyone missing but we should be diligent in our efforts", said Sara.

Flata said, "I want to check each member here to insure they are well and kicking. I am sure we are all in excellent health but I need to establish our parameters for future comparison."

The outer shield of the space craft which protects the craft when it is in transit near the speed of light, began to withdraw into their protective containers, leaving the cosmos in plain view. The blackness of space was dotted with shining diamonds and not far away a beautiful green and blue planet hung in the black velvet of space slowly rotating. There were no Icey poles as, or was, prevalent on the earth. The greenery extended into high mountains onto the misty shrouded peaks, tops not being visible. The blue water covered at least half of the planet and no doubt would present a desirable invitation to Muskula and her species.

Hopefully, future generations upon the new world would not present a problem with the land dwellers. Sara hoped it could be that way but knowing human nature and its propensity for violence, it did not seem like peaceful coexistence would be an option. They would have to find a different water world for Muskula and her people.

After everyone had regained consciousness and had greeted each of their friends, a bright flash lighted the entire, miles wide, enclosure. At first everyone was startled and had a spike of fear thinking that perhaps they had a new enemy which had struck first. Then, floating down thru the mist, they observed three figures. They were perplexed as to whom or what they could be and what they represented.

The three figures remained in the air just beyond their reach. Then everyone instantly recognized Emily Smith, Blain and Sasha. Perilain, Orion, and Warren Jr. each cried out. Perilain for his mother Sasha and Father Blain, and Orion for his Mother Emily and his father Blain and Warren Jr. just for his mother Emily, and of course Blain, as he was his father figure all the years, he was on the intergalactic carrier on which he was born.

"Oh! Families and friends. We are so proud of you. You did your duty as was requested by The Great Cosmic Spirit. You will be rewarded for you works. There are amazing things in store for you. However, you should not think of this new paradise as a retirement community. There are so many marvelous and wonderous adventures ahead just waiting for you to begin and experience. After you settle in the refugee populations on the New Earth, we will come back and instruct you to enable you to perform your new task. We need to find each and every seed carrier launched with our citizens and take them to their new home."

Emily quit speaking and smiled her lopsided smile, a lock of blonde hair hanging just above one eye. All three entered every mind caressing them with a loving embrace, Blaine and Sasha infusing warmth and love with special attention to their sons. The family stood in a trance receiving the small neurons of refreshment from their loved ones.

CHAPTER 53
THE LAST SUNRISE

Sara and Jawane stood on a high plateau overlooking the plains below. The new earth was absolutely beautiful. The most amazing and refreshing thing was the cool crispness of the air. It was slightly damp from the mist that hung in the small recesses of the plains. One could see a small stream meandering its way thru the bottom lands which was rich with green long stem grasses. The sun, having just recently risen above the horizon, gave the stream a brilliant silver and gold reflection as it wound its way thru the forest intermittently hidden from view with the dark green foliage.

"I think I could stay here forever Jawane but if I did, I do not think I would know what to do with myself. There should not be any need for the military here for years to come. I really cannot see myself planting corn. However, it would be nice to start a family, don't you think?"

Jawane was silent for several minutes as he was thinking the exact same thing.

"Yes, it would be nice. However, we could do the same thing on an Intergalactic Seed Carrier. It is a world unto itself. They are not as rigid and stringent now as when our parents came to the earth."

"Look Jawane, you can see a large group of people moving toward the base of the mountains. I think they will do fine. We chose the smartest and brightest of the population to start over. I wonder how they will judge us in the coming generations?"

Jawane was solemn. "Hopefully they will remember us without judgement. Sara, it is time to leave, let us begin our new journey".

And turning, they walked hand in hand and quietly returned to their saucer and left the New Earth after watching their last sunrise.

Below, on the plain, huge herds of all of Earths' mammals grazed in the lush grass. Flocks of geese circles the lakes. And, all things were good. It was indeed an Eden paradise.

TARGET EARTH

Thank You for reading the Emily Smith Trilogy. I hope they engaged your mind and will allow you to consider that we are not the only intelligence in this great universe. Good things are coming our way and perhaps have already arrived, we just are not ready to receive them yet. The adventures our decendents have will be exciting and awesome. Alliances will be made and their assistance will enable us to explore our solar system and develop the resources required for the next phase of our space faring adventures.

Most people who are serious about writing, start a writing career early in life. I wrote my first book, "Seed of Hope", at age sixty-eight. I finished my last book, "Target Earth", at age seventy-seven. Why would I write these particular genera of books? The things I have written about are things that I believe will come to pass in one form or another. But primarily, I write for my descendants. I have been blessed to see not only my grandchildren but four of my great grandchildren.

I wish I had a letter, a picture, or any small thing from my great grandparents, or any of my progenitors. I am sure that living their lives in the mid eighteen-hundreds and earlier was fraught with many challenges and heartaches. I imagine they would tremble in fear should they see our time. And no doubt we would tremble in fear to see into the future that our great grandchildren will face and the challenges they will have to overcome.

My next book will be dedicated to my Grandson and his adventures with a magical pony. Writing should be fun with a purpose in mind. I choose to be light and

positive. I would hope that my books at my age would encourage you to write your heart and perhaps help heal a soul along the way.
    Thomas Artie Turpen-Young
    Tom Young

CPSIA information can be obtained
at www.ICGtesting.com
Printed in the USA
JSHW081024050423
39931JS00002B/156